IN ORBIT

NOVELS BY WRIGHT MORRIS
IN BISON BOOK EDITIONS

Date of first publication at the left

A BISON BOOK

IN ORBIT

WRIGHT MORRIS

UNIVERSITY OF NEBRASKA PRESS
LINCOLN AND LONDON

Library of Congress Cataloging in Publication Data

Morris, Wright, 1910–
   In Orbit.

   "A Bison book."
   Reprint of the ed. published by New American Library, New York.
   I. Title.
[PZ3.M8346In4] [PS3525.07475] 813'.5'2   75–14359
ISBN 0–8032–5830–5

First Bison Book printing: 1976
Most recent printing indicated by first digit below.
1   2   3   4   5   6   7   8   9   10
Bison Book edition published by arrangement with
the author. Originally published in 1967 by the New
American Library, Inc.

IN ORBIT

CHAPTER ONE

This boy comes riding with his arms high and wide, his head dipped low, his ass light in the saddle, as if about to be shot into orbit from a forked sling. He wears a white crash helmet, a plastic visor of the color they tint car windshields, half-boots with stirrup heels, a black horsehide jacket with zippers on the pockets and tassels on the zippers, levis so tight in the crotch the zipper on the fly is often snagged with hair. Wind puffs his sleeves, plucks the strings of his arms, fills the back of his jacket like a wineskin, ripples the soot-smeared portrait of J. S. Bach on his chest. His face is black as the bottom-side of a stove lid, except for his nose, which is pewter-colored. He has the sniffles, and often gives it a buff with his sleeve. He is like a diver just before he hits the water, he is like a Moslem prayer-borne toward Mecca, he is like a cowpoke hanging to the steer's horns, or a highschool dropout fleeing the draft. If he resembles this the least it is understandable: it is what he is.

All of this can be taken in at a glance, but the important detail might escape you. He is in motion. Now you see him, now you don't. If you pin him down in time, he is lost in space. Between where he is from and where he is going he wheels in an unpredictable orbit. To that extent he is free. Any moment it might cost him his life. As he rides he sings "I Got You, Babe"—but he has no babe, worse he has no voice. The words of his song string out behind him like the tail of a kite. The fresh smear of road oil scents the air and his visor is smoked with road film. Underfoot hisses the adhesive rip of soft tar. The line down the center of the road is the zipper, and he is the zip. Yet he is doing no more than what comes naturally, if you'll admit that it takes talent. This he has. The supernatural is his natural way of life.

That's the picture. You might want to add a few details of your own. A few ribbons to the helmet, trailing like a jet's stream, or the boot tops worn with the suède side outside, or a windscreen smeared with the wings of gnats and honey-freighted bees. Across the back of the jacket might be studs of nickel, or gems that gleam in the lights like a road sign. The hair should be long, the levis short, the cuffs raggedly scissored and preferably frayed. But natural or supernatural the boy needs food, and the bike needs gas. Topping the rise he climbs, propeller-type banners twirl between the gas pumps of the One-Stop Diner. The woman hosing down the cinders glances up to watch him go by. She knows the type. She is puzzled why this one doesn't stop. They come from miles around to stop at the One-Stop Diner, not to whoosh past. From the han-

10

dlebars of motorbikes parked at the side dangle the tails of coons sold in auto-parts stores. They stopped to eat, they stopped for gas, they stopped to splatter ketchup on a plate of her French fries, to play the jukebox, to use the can and run a comb through their duck's ass hair-dos, their wind-glazed bloodshot eyes like those of beached fish. They stopped to stop. Having stopped made it possible to go. Pauline Bergdahl, safe between her gas pumps, wearing unlaced tennis sneakers and a surplus pea jacket, takes it all in, and then some, at a glance. Does she note something more than a favoring wind at his back? Something more than the usual spring in his legs? To the trained eye there's a difference between a boy on the go and one on the run. As he passes she flicks him with a spray from her hose, and the boom of his sound wave twirls the banners and presses the dangling bib of her apron between her lean thighs.

To the trained eye there's a difference between a boy on the go, and a boy on the run. Pauline Bergdahl admits as much to Curt Hodler when she gets to the phone and calls him.

"Mr. Hodler," she says, "he'd've stopped if he hadn't."

"Hadn't what?" says Hodler.

"Swiped it, Mr. Hodler. Some find it just too much trouble to lock it." Hodler makes no comment, so she adds, "Just remember they ain't a mean bunch, Mr. Hodler. Whatever else you can say, they ain't a mean bunch."

Whatever else Hodler can say, he has said many times. He is silent until the buzzing sound tells him that she has hung up. Thanks to her, however, it cannot be said that Hodler is a stranger to the type. They go by him on the highways, snorting like gas saws, they occupy the cushioned booths in the One-Stop Diner, they cluster like hoods around the phone booth and block the mirror in the lavatory, the air scented with their reefers, hair pomade, and saddle soap. Hodler has been in the war, and he would choose it again to facing them alone in a movie lobby. If they ain't a mean bunch, he is a simple coward at heart. He is also editor of the *Pickett Courier*, and will pay cash money for hot news tip-offs. Many of them come from Pauline Bergdahl, who knows the type. If the tip is a hot one Hodler will pay ten dollars. If it is a cold one he will pay five. In Pauline Bergdahl's case the issue is not so simple since her cold tips often prove to be hot ones. He can save five dollars by taking it cold. In her case, it is less a question of temperature than talent. Only Pauline Bergdahl would report, in passing, that a motorbike was squeaky new. If Hodler doesn't have the talent, over the years he has learned to have a little patience. With a little time Pauline Bergdahl's tips often proved to be hot.

Her specialties are fires and highschool dropouts, but she sometimes calls Hodler on neighborly matters. One is Holly Stohrmeyer. A neighbor of Pauline's, Miss Holly is a gentle, childlike woman, and like a child she loves to wander. She's not young, but no one can think of her as old. On a warm spring day she might just slip off and be gone for hours. It's the wandering that has led to problems, and why her people, when alive, moved into the country. It helped, of course, but it didn't stop it. As a rule one of her neighbors finds her dawdling along the road. The dogs love her, so she never goes far unchaperoned. On a warm springy day like this one she might make it all the way to Bergdahl's Corners, where Pauline would give her a glass of buttermilk or a cup of tea. Pauline has stopped giving her ice because of the way she sits and chews or sucks it. If Mr. Bergdahl is around he will drive her back home, or Pauline will call Hodler, or her guardian, Sanford Avery. She usually calls Hodler because Sanford Avery is not her type. He has more or less implied that Miss Holly wouldn't wander if people didn't reward her with so many free drinks.

There was a time, of course—and not so far back—when gentle simple-minded people like Holly Stohrmeyer found their proper place in a town like Pickett. The men could always help with the mail glut at Christmas, cut lawns and rake leaves, run the necessary errands: the women could help with the ironing and the sewing, help with the chores. Even today a simple fellow called Charlie shines most of the gentlemen's shoes in Pickett. Not the ladies', however. They are disturbed by his jokes, and the time it takes him to make change. At one time Miss Holly, too, had her place, and was in some demand as a babysitter. But these babies grew up, and she was not quite so good with the babies of the postwar generation. Perhaps they were smarter. Perhaps she had got a little less smart herself.

Since the war Hodler did his little bit to help settle, he has been the editor of the *Pickett Courier*. He works hard.

He does not cheat or gamble but he relies heavily on what is known as luck. The vague nature of this word is a solace to Hodler because he chooses most of his words with care. No one has ever heard him say, "As luck would have it"—but as luck would have it, he hears it all the time. Mrs. Bergdahl, for example, can seldom make her point without it. "As luck would have it, Mr. Hodler," she says, "I was there between the gas pumps, hosin' down the cinders, when—" Hodler knows better than argue the point. Nothing is less a matter of luck than the weather, but Hodler admits to the frailty of language. The forecast for today, for example, reads:

Friday, May 17th
Chance for rain 80%

As luck would have it the chances for rain, this time of year, are often better. But the forecast is less important than the date, May 17th. The date, strange to say, is more important in the long run than anything in the paper. Day in and day out the news is pretty much the same. All of it bad. Most of it soon forgotten. It is the date that gives it meaning. It makes more sense out of the news than Hodler can make. If, as luck would have it, anything of interest happens on this sultry May morning, Hodler will end up remembering the date. If a paper loses its dateline it loses its mind. The purpose of the forecast is to pin down the day, whether it rains or not.

Of Swiss ancestry, Hodler's big-knuckled hands are like bared roots, or grape stumps after pruning. He has never plucked a grape, or bared a root, but if you are *echt* Swiss you are born with such hands. If you are Hodler, you will never, no never, really train them to type. Nevertheless, he has managed to both write and type a book about the Swiss who shaped American culture. But little consolation it gives him. What, if any, *shape* has it? On Hodler's troubled mind's eye it seems a mindless force, like the dipping, dancing funnel of the twister, the top spread wide to spew into space all that it has sucked up. It is like nothing so much as the dreams of men on the launching pad. Or those boys who come riding, nameless as elemental forces, their arms spread wide and with coiled springs in their asses, ticking off the countdown they hope will blast them out of this world. A crippled, clod-footed species when not mounted on something, their legs bowed to fit their mechanical ponies, idle, loutish, but not—on one authority—a mean bunch at heart. Hardly a day passes, if Hodler is on the highway, he isn't hooted or buzzed by one of these phantoms, whooshing past him like a rocket about to take off. When they go by him everything is flapping, a penumbra of light vibrates around them. Where are they going? Even worse, where have they been? As luck would have it, Pauline Bergdahl often claims to know.

But on a morning like this one Hodler's first thought, hearing Pauline's voice, was of Miss Holly. He almost suggested he might stop by, and take her home. But Pauline had merely called to say that in her opinion it was twister weather, and while hosing down her cinders she had seen, just in passing, this boy on the swiped motorbike.

"Pauline," Hodler had said, "how you know he *swiped* it?"

"Mr. Hodler," she replied, "he'd've stopped if he hadn't."

That was half an hour ago. The wisdom of it still weighs on Hodler's mind. When the phone rings again he is almost certain he knows who it is, and says, "Pauline?"

But it is not Pauline. The hoarse voice brays, "Nope, this Avery. You alone, Hodler?"

Hodler is always alone, but out of habit he says, "How's Miss Holly, Avery?"

"Who the hell'd know that!" he croaks. Sanford Avery is Hodler's local weather beagle, an authority on early and late frosts, long dry spells, long wet spells, long hot and cold spells: if it's long on something it's Avery's. Hodler says, "What's the dope?"

"Can you get out here quick?"

That he sounds hoarse with panic does not disturb Hodler. Avery panics easily. He lives alone on a chicken farm with a woman who would tax any man's patience. "I'm callin' you before the Sheriff," he says. "How soon can you make it?"

"Miss Holly——?"

"She's been—attacked."

Hodler thinks of Bluestone's big police dog, Hank, he thinks of bees (the house is a hive) and he thinks of snakes. "By what?"

"Ah-tacked. Ah-*tacked!*" Avery whispers hoarsely to keep from shouting. "Ah-*tacked*, Hodler. She's been raped."

Hodler doesn't believe that for a moment. "It isn't something she thinks? Something she's just dreamed up?" The sound Avery makes is characteristic. A cross between a snorting neigh and a whinny. "Look—" Hodler says, "you've got to be sure. With something like this *we've* got to be sure."

"She tried to ward him off! She cut him. She cut herself."

Hodler knows the house: he can see Avery standing just left of the kitchen stove, facing the wall phone. His voice is like that of an old hound.

"You're sure?" Once more Avery whinnies. "I'll be right out, you hear me? Don't call *anybody* till I get there, you hear me?"

"She slashed him! There's blood on the knife!"

Hodler puts the phone in the cradle gently. If he doesn't hear the click Avery will go on talking, assuming that Hodler sits there listening. Living with a child has made him garrulous. It has finally made him mad. This does not come as a surprise to Hodler, but the manner of its coming is surprising. Miss Holly raped. Miss Holly slashing at somebody with a knife. What a light that cast into the darker corners of Avery's mind! Hodler shakes two aspirin from the bottle on his desk and rises to walk to the water cooler. His pants peel like a Band-Aid from the hardwood seat of his chair. The morning is already warm and sultry. May days that began like this often ended up in a blow. Pauline Bergdahl had already said so. An opinion that Sanford Avery would second. He would have said so himself if he had not lost what little mind he had.

Miss Holly *raped?* Hodler sees her always in the same velvet dress, the green beige faded to the color of a train seat, smooth as the stroked pelt of a cat on the seat and the lap. It went well with the upholstery on platform rockers, and helped to hold her to chairs with slippery covers. Her dangling ankles would be crossed: the corset propped her erect. The parents of very small or nursing children often had the problem that Miss Holly's velvet bust, so pneumatically ample, might be strewn with straight pins and needles that dangled a teasing length of thread. These hazards never troubled Miss Holly, but they often punctured the younger children. They did it deliberately, since it was known that she would kiss anything that bleeds or hurts.

When Hodler came to Pickett he would often see her, trailing a two-wheeled cart, doing the Stohrmeyer shopping. She had a list. She often did the shopping for people who were busy, like Curt Hodler. She bought his aspirin, his razor blades, and the Red Cross cough drops he ate like candy. She was good with money. In the moist palm of her hand even old dirty coins looked new. Hodler was not one of the first, however, to learn of Miss Holly's problem. She was shoplifting. Someone phoned it in as a hot news tip.

Along with all those goodies she would put into her cart, there were countless others she slipped into her pockets. Without exception they came in small tins and bottles: they were little things. She seemed to find anything that was small enough hard to resist. That included pills, perfumes, and cosmetics, bottles of saccharine, deodorants, vanilla extract. Pills and vanilla extract soon run into money. But there were ways to deal with the money angle. What proved impossible to handle was Miss Holly's passion to give it all to children. Aspirin, Band-Aids, dental floss, nail polish, and especially a wide selection of lipsticks. Lipsticks were things most small fry could appreciate. Hodler often saw them, painted like Indians, holding a powwow in the playground, their mouths stuffed with Miss Holly's free packets of Feenamint or chlorophyll gum.

From Hodler's window she might be mistaken for one of them. Her face is round and smooth, she has a child's serene unblinking gaze. She is pretty as a child. The freckled nose has not emerged from her face. Someone has likened her to a doll with a real wig. From the rear, however, and down on her own level, she resembles a cello in a snug velvet case. Her hair is worn in the long tight braids that occupy her hands most of the morning. These small hands, pudgy as a child's, absent-mindedly move across her gaze for wisps of hair that cling to her lips, or comb the vacant air near her face for invisible strands. This gesture suggests a child's long, long thoughts. There is nothing, no nothing, to suggest the woman somebody will rape. Hodler's pity for her is compounded of pity for himself. If the needle hadn't skipped in the making of Miss Holly—a stitch somewhere dropped, or perhaps one knotted—it is probable, if not likely, that Hodler would not now be a bachelor. Nor Miss Holly Stohrmeyer, if Avery proved to be right, assaulted and raped. Wouldn't it be Hodler, of all people, to inquire, "And how is Miss Holly?"

For more than twenty years Avery's cynical answer had been the same. *Who the hell would know that?* Now thanks to some snooping idler, or passing stranger, that was no longer an idle question. Somebody finally knew. It is a torment to Hodler that this essential knowledge is what he once desired for himself. How *was* Miss Holly. Some idle lecher, some wandering pervert, some bored delinquent, some loyal friend or guardian, envied but unknown to Hodler, and still at large, finally knew.

CHAPTER TWO

From his father he has the name Jubal, and a baseless pride. The name Gainer can be found on sheds near the river and the bottoms of hexagonal hair-tonic bottles. They can be used to store whiskey for medicinal purposes. His grandfather went to prison for an honest crime, but they let him off with a dishonorable pardon. From his mother he has an ear for music and the green in his eyes.

His closest friend is Harry Elmo Radich, a Ringo-type drummer and quiet beer drinker. His farthest friend is LeRoy Cluett, who is old enough to buy and drink package likker. They are all dropouts from Olney County high school and planned to fight and win the war together. Then LeRoy Cluett bought himself a set of barbells and a hernia. On the strength of this hernia he got himself a wife and a new motorbike.

They can draft you in Olney County but you have to get to Muncie to be inducted. That's why it was that Jubal came riding with his arms around LeRoy Cluett's fat waist, his ass heavy on the cushion at the rear of LeRoy's new motorbike. Modern global warfare being what it is they planned to first pick up some girls and take in a good movie. Modern Indiana girls being what they are they settled for William Holden and Mickey Rooney. William Holden had the mission of bombing the bridges of Toko-Ri. These bridges, as they took pains to show, were over a river in a narrow, barren canyon. The big screen of the movie made it easy to see how treeless it was. There were no holes to crawl into, there was no place to hide. When his mission was accomplished William Holden didn't crash, or return to his carrier to receive a medal, but instead all he did was run out of gas. He came down in this country without any trees, and without any gas. The United States Navy came to his rescue but except for Mickey Rooney they all flew off and left him. They had the planes, they had the fire power, but they didn't have the gas. Not that Jubal really believed it. He waited for the Navy to come flying back. He was fully prepared for their shooting Mickey Rooney, as he was prepared for their shooting LeRoy Cluett, but he was not prepared for their leaving William Holden all alone in China. LeRoy Cluett dead, Harry Radich in the Peace Corps, Jubal Gainer all by himself.

In Jubal's opinion an army was an army with millions of fighting men, three or four of them your buddies, and sick leave with nurses. A navy was a navy with thousands of ships and sailors, several weeks of shore leave, and plenty of good air cover. It was not a bunch of goddam gas-eating jets that would run out of gas. It was not one poor goddam gob left to die in a ditch. He didn't buy it. It was not at all his idea of war. Even worse, it was not at all his idea of a just peace. The face of war that he knew and believed in was Sinatra and his pals fighting and winning it together, screwing the girls, then coming home to enjoy the peace. He was no fool, he knew war was hell, but nobody had told him it was crazy. Nobody had told him it was up to Jubal if he ran out of gas.

Long stories sometimes take very little time. First they went to this movie, then they picked up some cigars and lay around drinking beer like they were on shore leave. Both LeRoy and Jubal were more accustomed to cigars, being ten months older than Harry and freer with their money. LeRoy was more accustomed to package likker and the good points of foreign-type women. If Jubal was more the tall type, like William Holden, LeRoy was more along the lines of Mickey Rooney, and without the hernia he might have made a good Marine. He claimed to be very horny and liked to talk about the women he'd laid. The motel cabin they were in was mostly used by moochers who mussed up the towels but hardly got the sheets dirty. Jubal lay on his back smoking one of LeRoy's three-for-fifty cigars. He inclined to spit a lot when he smoked cigars, and took a lid from the stove and used the hole to spit in. So did LeRoy. They used the bottom of the lid to scrounge out the butts.

Jubal was not exactly beer drunk, nor was he really cigar sick, but it had something to do with the way he was feeling, and what he happened to say. What he happened to say was that for a man so horny, LeRoy Cluett had a very small horn. A simple fact. After all, he had seen it often enough.

After a moment LeRoy said, "You're a smart kid, Gainer," and gave his cigar a twist on the sooty stove lid. "You're a smart kid, you know that? You'd make a good straight man in a minstrel show."

Naturally Jubal asked him just what the hell it was he meant by that? LeRoy gave his cigar another twist on the stove lid, then held it up like a brush dipped in stoveblack. "If that pimply puss of yours was black," he said, "you'd make it big, like Sammy Davis."

Jubal retorted that between a very small horn and pimples—even if they were black ones—he would settle for the pimples. LeRoy seemed to take that quiet enough. He belched, then he got up to pee in the washbowl sink in the corner. All Jubal said was that for a man so low to the ground he ought to use the can. Another simple fact. For a boy both so low, and so fat-assed, LeRoy Cluett was fast. Before Jubal could move LeRoy had him straddled with his legs trapped under the covers. His wide fat ass was on Jubal's chest, his thighs squeezing his head. "You're an awful smart kid, Gainer," he said, and rubbed the sooty cigar butt into Jubal's face, using it like a brush around his eyes and mouth, screwing it into his ears and up his nose. "All you need's a black eyepatch," he said, and gave him a poke in one eye. Then he just sat on him awhile, touching up the light spots, using the stove lid as a palette and the cigar butt as a paintbrush. He added some touches to the portrait on Jubal's chest. Then he rolled off Jubal and went into the bathroom, locking the door. Jubal could hear the shower drumming on the tin wall. He could hear him sing. He got up to take a look at his face in the mirror, and it was neither Sammy Davis nor was it Jubal Gainer. Who then? The mouth seemed small for so many white teeth. The sooty smear of stoveblack stopped at the hairline so that he looked like a minstrel with a shrinking wig. But it taught him something. The pimples on his forehead hardly showed. The black eye that LeRoy had just given him hardly showed. But knowing who he really was was not the same as recognizing himself.

First he thought he would burn LeRoy's clothes in the stove but it takes a hot fire to burn leather. The leather jacket was black with a lamb's-wool lining and tasseled zippers on the pockets. The crash helmet that hung on the stovepipe damper wouldn't burn at all. LeRoy Cluett was short and fat-assed but he proved to have the same hat-size as Jubal. Jubal had never owned a helmet. Neither had he owned a jacket with a lamb's-wool lining, both so short in the sleeves and so roomy in the shoulders. How did it look? Steam from the shower filmed the bureau mirror. Jubal did not wipe a hole in the film to look at himself. In the pocket of the jacket he found a pack of Kools, seven dollars in bills, and the keys to the Suzuki. With the helmet on his head he could almost hear himself think. Did he make a decision? Not that he knew of. It was LeRoy Cluett who had made it for him. All Jubal had to do was what LeRoy would do, or Harry Radich would do, in the same situation. After all, it came naturally to him, as it would to them. A bad soldier is a dead one. A good soldier is one who runs for his life.

When he stepped out of the cabin the signs on the

freeway were like the names on moving freight cars. Too many. He went in the direction the bike would coast. There was sand where the ice filmed the road in the winter making a sound like a wire brush stroking the fenders. The night passed, peeling his shadow from the reeling road. At the side of it the wires dipped and rose, with a lapping sound the poles flag him. Is he in orbit? A burst of flak brings him down. The gunner stands on an island between two gas pumps, the flak slaps like hail on his helmet. A moment later the motor coughs, like a sick calf. Coming toward him, shadow-dappled, is a small red car that seems to run without a driver. A plane spraying the orchards skims the treetops, trailing a plume that sprinkles his visor. The tongue he puts to his lips tastes of soot. The bike coasts, in a soundless vacuum, toward a post propped in a milk can, a single mailbox on the rim of the wagon wheel. He coasts to where he can read the name Stohrmeyer on its side. Little wonder he has come flying hell-for-leather with the road spinning beneath him like a ribbon of asphalt. His bombed bridges are behind him. Like William Holden he is on his own now, and out of gas.

▪

In matters of gas Charlotte Hatfield knows that her husband, Alan, runs out of it, and that Haffner does not. In neither case would she know where the gas was put, or what became of it. Such details are not the ones she takes in at a glance. With her nearsighted eyes, Charlotte's impression is vivid in proportion to its vagueness. If it is vague, there is more room in it for Charlotte. Like the cat in her lap, wrapped in a purple guest towel, Charlotte will hear the mouse in the floor, not the plane on the roof. She will see, wherever she looks, what little she likes. The roaring object coming toward her on the road, for example, is like a golf ball driven toward the lens of her camera, the helmet ballooning larger and larger to where she could see the face painted on it—or was it trapped inside? A mask, surely. Hardly what she would call a face. As for the overall impression of the boy on the bike, it is that of two cats, piggyback: hard at it. She sees what she knows, this Charlotte, and she knows cats. She knows or thinks she knows the man at her side. His name is Haffner. He drives her around since she doesn't drive. A small man, he sits so low in the seat the car appears to be running by itself. Many get that impression. Often it proves to be accurate. In his absorption, or his excitement, or sometimes just his total indifference, Haffner will occasionally forget that the car needs his attention. He came to driving late: in Alan Hatfield's opinion, too late. Those who come to it late, Alan says, never really make it. They never trust it. They've no idea why it stops or goes. That is why little Haffner leans forward, pushing, when his foot presses the starter. It is why he leans back, pulling, when he hopes it will stop. He is constantly debating with it. "Now what is it you're up to? Here? Now look!" In slow traffic he tries to shake it. On the open road he forgets it. His foot is now on, now off, the gas pedal: he plays the brake like a piano. The view in the rearview mirror interests him more than the front. Why not? That is always where he gets hit. He has himself struck nothing unless rudely propelled from behind. Charlotte does not drive, she does not fly, she prefers not to walk: this leaves a good deal in the hands of the people who know her, in particular Felix Haffner. The gas is his problem. The cat in her lap is hers.

Her husband, Alan, has nothing special against cats, but when they are sick he hasn't much going for them. This one is sick. Too many fleas, worms, and an abscessed ear. Haffner is neutral in the matter of cats unless they are sick and belong to Charlotte Hatfield. There have been many, thanks to the fact that she likes them non-fixed.

Charlotte's cats average a trip to the vet about every two months. Getting them to the vet is the big problem since Charlotte likes Dr. Crowe, over in Elvira, rather than Dr. Kleeber in the suburbs of Pickett. This one hisses at Dr. Kleeber with a sound like a bathroom deodorizer. Charlotte is sure he couldn't do that if he was fixed. Because he is non-fixed, this one also sprays the fireplace and the white sidewalls on Alan's Porsche. His name is Morgan. Alan would also like to see him fixed—but for good. Not just de-flea'd and repaired every two or three months.

Alan Hatfield writes and teaches poetry, with a seminar in the modern verse drama. Haffner teaches French, the German novel, and gives a drama course in the existential theater, where he and his students participate in what are called "happenings." Things just happen. No reason, no reason, just a happening. It is as hard for Alan to participate in these affairs as it is easy and pleasurable for Charlotte. He can't seem to get with it. Charlotte just seems to be with it naturally. In Alan's opinion, however, this does not excuse Charlotte's using Haffner as a chauffeur for herself and Morgan. Alan always says Morgan. He does not want to imply it is more than that.

Not only does Charlotte not drive a car, but having no driver's license she cannot cash a check. She can only cash checks where people know her, and few do. Nearly all of Charlotte's checks come back to Alan with Felix Haffner's weird scrawl on their backs, as large and ragged as he is small and elegant. *He* knows her. If she's asked, it is Haffner who remembers her own phone number. Charlotte still can't forget the one they had in Santa Monica, and she still wishes she had it. There's no number in Pickett she can ever remember, especially her own. It also disturbs Alan to have *all* of Charlotte's checks going through so many hands with Haffner's name scrawled on them, but what can she do? It is Haffner who knows her. Besides if he has nothing better to do than chauffeur her to Elvira, that is his business. He has said so countless times. Problems of this magnitude rest lightly on Charlotte but they add up to a burden for Alan. If he says, "I'll be damned if I know what to do—" she will instantly reply, "Me neither." Why should that unnerve him? Why should it silence him for hours? Haffner, on the other hand, will make the same remark just to hear Charlotte's usual answer. He laughs as if he judged it witty.

People who fall in love and are still in it when they marry are due for surprises, and Alan has had them. "You're going to think I'm peculiar when you know me," she had said. That was more than a year *after* they were married. At that time they were living in Perugia where the landlady thought Charlotte was an actress in hiding. Charlotte is beautiful as well as peculiar, and both are something of a strain for a man like Alan, but a greater strain would be life without her. He knew that. She knew that. After five years of marriage it is still a simple fact that if Alan *ever* knows her, he's going to think her peculiar. Not that it troubles Charlotte. Knowing people is not at all important if you're in love with them.

Charlotte developed her interest in cats in Rome, where their *crimes passionels* were taken for granted. When Alan pointed out where this might lead she cried out, "How would you like somebody to fix you, Mr. Smarty?" It was idle to argue the nice points about the word *fix*. One of the things Charlotte adores about Morgan is the view from the rear, since he has no tail. His endowment is heart-shaped. She cannot imagine him without it.

Charlotte is thirty-one, -two, or -three, depending on the season and the situation. When they are bad, she looks it. She is two years older than Alan, but she often looks as much as five years younger. Is it her fault that he looks so old because he looks so far ahead? Charlotte is dark, of an olive complexion, and in France they took her for Italian, in Italy for Greek. In all countries the men are happy to take her as she is. Until she went to France she thought her legs were expensive because of how quickly she went through her stockings. Her legs are no longer than the usual long legs, but somehow few women walk them, or cross them, like Charlotte. Can she help that? Charlotte likes some of France, most of Europe, and nearly all of Italy very much, but she is also reasonably happy to live with Alan in a place like Pickett. Nor does she want to be more than reasonably happy. It would be too much.

Charlotte is friendly with people, but inclined to be uninhibited. Alan has explained to her countless times the importance of inhibitions in civilized life, and that without them the people of Pickett would be like a bunch of middle-aged delinquents. Charlotte knows that. But there are days she simply prefers the delinquents, middle-aged or not. In Pickett this is usually Sunday and the sight of people eating in the Pickett Inn. They go to church just to work up an appetite, Charlotte says. They come from miles around just to sit near the windows so that people out driving can see them eating. Do they do anything but eat? When she says anything, she means *any*thing. They made reservations four months in advance for Easter Sunday and Mother's Day dinners, eating forty large cartons of instant spuds and more than thirty large sacks of frozen peas. A boy who worked in the kitchen supplied her with the figures.

Alan could only sympathize, then go on to point out that eating like pigs kept them out of worse mischief. They weren't out killing people on the state's highways, or in concentration camps. That argument carried little weight with Charlotte, based, as it was, on reason. In California, where they met and married, there was always the beach to go to on Sundays, although, as a matter of fact, they seldom went. Just knowing it was there seemed to be enough.

On the way to Elvira, Charlotte will often tell Haffner

what she has been dreaming. She dreams in color. It is what she tells people when they ask her why she doesn't write or paint. Her good dreams come toward morning, are very vivid, and prove to be color-fast until she tells them to Haffner, after which they fade. What is the meaning of that? Haffner doesn't seem to know, for the life of him. Even Alan lets his coffee cool in the morning to puzzle over the dream that Charlotte tells him. It resists analysis. It is a torment to Alan, a man who thinks. Like all of her non-fixed cats, Charlotte merely dreams to dream. If she had a tail, Haffner tells her, it would surely twitch.

When Alan says there is no accounting for tastes, Charlotte is the first to remind him that he should be grateful. Otherwise how explain his love for her, her love for him? Alan is masculine but gentle. He is reasonable but incomprehensible. All of which hardly matters since what she likes is the way he looks. In California Alan's brow was like a new copper penny and with oil on his skin he looked good enough to eat. She had thought his eyes green, but here in Indiana they prove to be the color of the season. In the summer smoky gray, in the winter amethyst. She has always loved the way his hair, on the beach, dries to his scalp like a seal's pelt. You see hair like that on teenage boys who are going to grow big. Until his hair is dry, with the lick protruding, Alan may look more Roman than Nordic, and there is often sand in the creases of his large ears. These are the small details Charlotte remembers from their first week together on the beach. Every night there was scratchy sand in their bed. Most of

Charlotte's tan, and all of her sun lotion, rubbed off on the sheets.

There's no accounting for tastes, but even Charlotte knows she has to stretch things a bit to account for Haffner. In point of fact, he is more AC than DC, and he could hardly care less for Charlotte, the sex kitten, well known for the whistles she gets from growing Pickett boys. Strangers in Pickett, seeing Haffner in his car, often take him for a spry, sporting widow, thanks to his addiction to colorful, imported Basque berets. They have pompons until they are lost, then turn up like bunny-tails in his pockets. He wears spats, matching gloves, a reversible topcoat with the tweed side out, a muffler that hangs to where he trips on the tassels or is looped like a cummerbund around his waist. Soiled cravats, off-white or baby-blue, support his head like an object in a jeweler's window. This elegance is invariably at odds with his stubble beard. No one will believe it, but he simply forgets to look in a mirror. A disturbing note is the way his hair has been worn thin in patches. It might be from the way he tosses at night: it might be the beret. With the free time on his hands during the yearly vacations Haffner represents a top line of imported Swiss chocolate, English toiletries for men, and French perfumes for women. The chocolate goes over big, but Charlotte ends up with most of the perfume. She wears it now. It clouds the oversweet fragrance of the Pickett spring.

Haffner does everything the *old* way, stalling Pickett noon traffic while he walks around the car to open the door for Charlotte. This is no idle gesture, since she can seldom open it for herself. There is a cat in her lap, or the handle on the door works the wrong way. Not infrequently Haffner will forget about the handbrake and the car will idle down the street, Haffner trailing, calling aloud *Here! Here!* as if to some unleashed pet. In such a crisis Charlotte is calm, secure in her belief that the car knows what it is doing. It is Haffner at the *wheel* that gives her the willies, not trailing along behind.

As Haffner came to driving so he came to English: late, too late. His voice is high, tilting to a shrill. He speaks four languages well, but he inclines to speak them all at once. It may explain why Charlotte listens intently to whatever he says. Her lips are parted. There is a narrowing of her dark eyes. What is he saying? Where, she wonders, does it all come from? His head is small, and she often feels that it is full of spools of very fine wire, thousands of spools. No end to the length of wire. When Charlotte plucks at one end she feels it might unravel forever. She rides with her eyes turned to the window, where she sees a dim reflection of the talking Haffner. He is always jabbering, recalling something, with no interest at all in where they are going. Charlotte has the interest but not much sense of place. They have seen a good deal of the country around Pickett. Little Haffner cares about the time lost, since he doesn't really believe in time. Time, he says, is for people who live on the installment plan. Yesterday already seems as near and as far as his childhood.

If Charlotte's pleasure in Haffner needs no explanation—she likes him because she likes him—his pleasure in her is more elusive. It has to do with his past. It has to do with the word "domesticated." Charlotte has been trained to live in a house, to use her box, and to purr when petted. But like the cat in her lap, she is a creature who has not been fixed.

When Haffner buzzed the bell this morning, for example, she cried out HAFFNER!, like a bingo winner. It is not what you'd call sensible, but it's Charlotte. Nor is it only for Haffner. After five years of marriage such impulsive behavior is still a cross for Alan. If Charlotte sees him on the street, or the steps of the P.O., or inserting a coin into a parking meter, she will let out a hoot. With her nearsighted eyes she is not infrequently mistaken. It isn't Alan at all. Too often it is someone who takes days to recover. Charlotte is often embarrassed, but she remains non-fixed.

From Pickett to Elvira is about twelve miles, but not often the way that Haffner drives it. Not that he is lost, but he is usually preoccupied. Going to Elvira is sometimes quite an adventure since it is always new and strange to Charlotte. In a moment she will cry out, "Did we go by it?", since she has no sense of distance. She is always amazed how they got there so soon, or why it took so long. "Was *that* there?" she will ask. It is a white barn with a silo. It had to have been there, of course, but she thinks it was not. It leads her to wonder aloud if they might be lost. One out of three times, roughly, they are. Haffner will then drive until he finds a gas station with the colors that match those on his credit card, charge five gallons, get his windshield wiped, and ask where he is. It is often Elvira. Not infrequently the gas-station attendant knows the place they are looking for. "You run your window down, bub," he says to Haffner, "an' you can hear 'em bark."

This morning Haffner drives with the windows cranked up to keep the bees out of the cab. One bee is enough. Charlotte's concern is equally divided between the bee and herself. Alan has explained that if a bee stings you, it pays with its life. The combination, all bad, is more than Charlotte can bear. With the windows up the cab smells of French perfume and English saddle leather. Haffner wears the paste on his shoes, the lotion on his face. Perhaps Charlotte thinks of the cat in her lap, since she is silent, her red lips parted. Several hairpins already lie in her lap. The hair she put up, just for Haffner, will soon come down. It is Alan who likes her to wear her hair up, but it is Haffner who dotes on the back of her neck. Is it something special? A turn-of-the-century Viennese neck. Clean for one thing, not at all like those so sadly exposed in existential drama, the earlobes dirty, rings worn by the tug and pull of cheap beads. Haffner has his standards, and it is Charlotte who has the neck. Although not a great beauty, Haffner's mother passed on an admirable neck to her talented daughters, all but one of whom, sawing their violins, bruised it horribly. That one played the harp, bruising only what might have been her bust. These prodigious children were already famous by the time little Haffner joined the ensemble, winning attention and applause for the way he turned the music on the racks. Soon enough the cumbersome cello was put in his hands. Led into the salon, perfumed with women, his sober sister Claudia serene at the piano, little Haffner would fuss with the strings of his bow, fuss with his chair, fuss with his music, prove to be a perfectionist with his tuning, then surrender to what was described as a spell of nerves. A sip of water he needed, powder on his moist hands, a lozenge for the nagging tickle in his throat, while the sober Claudia, as if stoned, sat with her small clenched fists in her lap, the bruise on her throat even darker than usual. "That little Haffner!" people said. Whatever they meant, it made him worse. He would do, and soon did, anything for a laugh. If he was not much of a performer, he was surely talented as an actor. He showed special promise as a clown.

At another time and another place—which might serve as a summary of his life—he might have made a great fool or influential court jester, cunningly shaping the lives of kings and empires, but Vienna, in 1913, was not the time. Kings and empires, at the moment, were tumbling down. Haffner did what he could to escape internment as the boy who turned the music for his gifted sisters, carried their violins, and went along when they needed a chaperone. If there was no question but what the girls had the talent, it was openly admitted that Haffner had the looks. A great pity, however, that his resemblance to Disraeli is lost on Charlotte.

Charlotte has seen many pictures of the Haffner ménage, gathered with their harps, cellos, and violas da gamba, but to tell the truth she finds them all a bit peculiar. They remind her of a group of touring midgets.

Nor does it help for Haffner to remind her they are prodigies. Little she cares. They look peculiar to her with their kinky hair, buggy eyes, and swollen foreheads. It is also strange how they resemble Haffner, yet he has the looks. All have the beak-like Haffner nose, and the wide lipless mouth, disturbingly chimp-like. And how can Haffner say that the eldest, as he so often does, reminds him of Charlotte? The bruise shows on her neck. She has a pigeon's bust. Charlotte's face is heart-shaped, her eyes are like almonds, and this is not the place to speak of her figure. Haffner wouldn't himself. He means that Sophia is his *favorite* sister, as well as being not a little peculiar. She is subject, unpredictably, to coming unglued. In the midst of an important recital, for example, Sophia might repeat the phrase of a sonata, over and over, like a needle stuck in its groove. Is it intentional? It is often hilarious. Perfectly sober and sensible music lovers will giggle and laugh. All that seems certain is that this disorder, if that is what it is, seems to run in the family. This flaw has been described as a nervous disturbance of the sort that resists treatment. A splintered nerve in the mind, a circuit shortened, something to do with the ends of the nerves, or the fingertips. In Haffner, perhaps, something to do with the end of the line.

Of less importance than where Haffner got it, is that he has it. Did he acquire it from his sister? It has gone far to pervert his taste. Although his knowledge of music is deep, he has come to prefer the flawed performance. The records that delight him are those where the needle skips a groove. More is gained, in his opinion, than the notes that are lost. It is the flaw that breaks the tiresome groove of the music in his mind. Once more he can hear it. Once more it is unpredictable.

If Haffner is cornered he will have to admit that he is bored by what the others love in the music. The fact that they *know* it: that it is predictable as rain. It cannot be explained, but the grain of such music goes against the grain of Haffner. Sometimes he could scream: not infrequently he does. When fate comes knocking at Beethoven's door, Haffner could batter it down. *Da-da-BAM!* he goes, coming down with both hands. It is good that his sisters were the ones with the talent or he might have tried his hand at composing. What stuff it would have been! Sonatas for one needle in, one out of the groove. Haffner has a small but select collection of records that are flawed in an original manner. The predictable fails: something not anticipated takes its place. Nor is this little quirk in Haffner's taste entirely confined to music. It can be seen in his own non-predictable behavior, and his non-fixed friends. It is what he likes about these pointless plays, these "happenings." What next? God only knows. Few things, for instance, give Haffner more delight than the flaws in Hodler's daily weather forecast. Is it weather, he asks, if you can forecast it? God knows what he means. In any case, the predictable bores him. He is made ill by the forecasts of polls. It was a sad day he discovered that a phonograph record is not a collection of grooves, but one groove only, spiraling toward its core. A clever analyst might suggest that he feels himself trapped. Little Haffner, a diamond-point needle stuck in such a groove.

Obviously, it has something to do with his own highly unpredictable behavior. Take the way he laughs. Anything at all might set it off. A newspaper headline, an astronaut in space, a memorable pronouncement by the nation's great leader, Hodler's daily weather forecast, or Pauline Bergdahl casually hosing down the cinders in front of her diner. Is that so funny? So much depends on your point of view. It might be the lowness of the water pressure, or the way she stands, spread-legged, dawdling with the nozzle. In any case it sets Haffner to laughing: his gloved hands slap the wheel. While he laughs the car is more or less obliged to steer itself. Haffner's eyes, brimming with laugh tears, are too blurred to see. Charlotte has found that he is like a child who makes the tears in his eyes do double duty. First he weeps, then with a kiss, or a conniving glance, he laughs. A sensible person can only wait for him to run down. He is like Charlotte, however, in the way he will toot his silly horn at half the people he passes, whether he knows them or not. It is Charlotte, of course, who waves at Pauline. Water from the wagging hose falls on the windshield with a splash.

Haffner's foot thumps the gas pedal and the racing motor vibrates the windshield. It gives a nervous animation to Pauline Bergdahl and the shimmering gas pumps. In a moment, Charlotte feels, they might leap and dance. The situation that often sets Haffner to laughing is one that might set Charlotte to dancing. She dances where

Haffner laughs. Just like that. She loves to dance with her Alan, who is quite good, and they make a very attractive couple, but there are times when she prefers to dance by herself. Alan has said,

> My baby needs no launching pad
> Kid Ory puts her
> In orbit.

The long slide and wail of Kid Ory's horn do, in fact, put Charlotte in orbit. Haffner, among others, has seen her twirling in the flagstone patio that is wired for music. Where is Alan? If you look closely you will see him inside. Somebody has to take charge of the record player and handle with care the old Kid Ory records. Somebody not in orbit has to lower the needle carefully into the groove. How it hisses and crackles! If it skips a groove somebody has to be there to give it a nudge. Most of these records have seen better days, and Alan has hinted that is also true of himself. But he is careful not to suggest it is true of Charlotte. It would be like saying the dancer is older than the dance.

If it is understood that life imitates art, the art of Haffner has dispensed with the imitation. He finds it wherever he looks, ready-made. On the shade side of the One-Stop Diner, for example, the motorbikes are parked like ponies at a hitchbar. A gentle breeze wags their real coon tails. One appears to be grazing in the dusty roadside weeds. As the Huns were once believed to be part of their horses, these riders look to Haffner like part of their machines. Gas percolates in their veins. Batteries light up their eyes. Carburetors have replaced their nervous systems. As for their brains, look for them on the dashboard, in the flicking dials. If they do not have the power of life, they have the power of death and exercise it. The bike would like to have a real tail, and wag it: the rider would like to be a real bike, and gun it. One day the bike would turn to nibble the grass, while the boy took on gas. When this new breed of creature was perfected the one stop at the diner would be a short one. The model would feature interchangeable parts. A bulb taken from the headlamp would screw into the eye. A glance at the dials would report what was on its mind. Haffner once dreamed of a petrol ballet, with lyrics by himself, the music by Stravinsky, a modern rites of spring chuffing and huffing with pistons, farting clouds of poisonous gas. He had the dream, but he lacked the talent. Haffner has terrified Charlotte with the notion that the really stupid will soon live forever, since an ignition system will suitably replace their worn-out parts. Why does he do this? It has passed his litmus test for truth. The very thought of it scares him to death.

Predictably Charlotte cries, "Did we go by it, Haffner?" but unpredictably they have not gone by it. The traffic snarl at the front of the clinic has made it impossible. Cars block the road. The air is blue with their exhausts. Haffner is delighted to see the healthy dogs with their ailing owners on leashes. His face beams with a lipless smile. The world has proved to be larger, but hardly stranger, than the Haffner salon on Florianigasse, where the predictable so often proved to be unpredictable.

Charlotte has managed to get out of the car without him. He runs the window down to hear what she is saying. "You don't need to wait," she cries, "I'll call Alan." With one arm she waves—one would think he was arriving—with the other, like a doll, she hugs the sagging Morgan, his rear legs dangling and his eyes bugging glassily. The scar of an old wound, hairless, rips the vest-like neatness of his underpelt, with its symmetrical buttons, reminding Haffner of some elegant ridiculous dandy trussed up to be knifed.

Does that sadden him? With reason. Under his topcoat he sports a garment not unlike it. Eight buttons. No larger, to the eye, than the teats of a cat.

Just a moment ago Haffner was laughing and happy: now he is sad. His bird-like animation, which so many find tiresome, is that of a canary in a sunny upper window. He sings if someone is listening. Otherwise not a peep. Left alone in his bug of a car he is the bird in a cage that is hooded. He chirps not one chirp: hops not one hop. The merry jester, in an instant, is the melancholy fool.

The dark side of Haffner's temperament is no surprise to wiseacres, analysts, widows, psychologists, and Charlotte, but it is always and forever a surprise to Haffner. What can he do? He has found that it helps to eat. Anything that he knows he *shouldn't* eat, and eats, proves to be a help.

At a roadside fruitstand droning with bees he buys a quarter-pound sack of forbidden Bing cherries. Are they so perilous? Haffner chews, sucks, cracks, and often swallows the pits. It can't be helped. A passion is a passion, as Charlotte says. The sack open in his lap, the juice red on his lips, he rides with the perfumed wind in his face. Bees crawl in his lap. Into the breeze he spits an occasional stone. On others he chews to get the bitter, wormy aftertaste of Kirsch. A drizzle-like sprinkle films the windshield from the plane that flies low, spraying the orchards. Through the smear left by the wiper Haffner sees an object gleaming like a road sign. Why does it look familiar? It proves to be a white crash helmet. Haffner comes up and goes by before he recalls where he saw it before. The kid on the motorbike: the piggyback monster with the carburetor lungs and the blinkers for eyes. Is it because the boy doesn't turn and thumb a ride that Haffner is inclined to make an exception? He jams his foot on the brake; he gives a toot on the horn. The boy comes up slowly, waddling like a cowpoke, dangling at his side a green army duffle that sweeps the ditch grass. The frayed bottoms of his levis are no longer tucked in his boots. Sweat darkens the portrait of J. S. Bach on his chest. This last detail is not lost on Haffner: as he cranks down the window he says, "Out of gas?"

The helmet framed in the window seems to have no face. An amber visor screens the eyes, out of the shadow a nose slowly emerges. Is it of pewter? The color is fading around the wide mouth. It is like nothing Haffner has ever seen, but it does not go beyond what he has often

44

imagined. A white man emerging from a black man, or the two in one. A man who makes the most, or is it the least, of a color-fast situation. Better yet, a man whose colors, madras-style, are guaranteed to bleed. Haffner can only laugh: he laughs in the boy's dark two-toned face.

But there is no malice in it. He takes from his lap the bag of cherries and thrusts it toward him. The hand the boy extends toward the bag has three white knuckles and two black ones. What can Haffner do but laugh until he chokes? His head dips down, he is doubled up with laughter, when the boy takes the bag and crowns him with it: fits it, that is, snugly to his head, then comes down hard on it with the flat of his hand. The bag pops, the cherry juice runs, and the little car drifts as if somebody has pushed it. Inside it Haffner's head lolls on the wheel and he snorfels like a man who is gasping for air. One would have to say, if that was how he was found, that he had laughed to death. Little the boy who crowned him with the cherries seems to care. He watches the car drift down the road to a bend where it slips into a ditch rank with weeds and water. The air above it is threaded with the glistening needles of dragonflies. Haffner continues to whimper, but whoever finds him will first lend an ear to the idling motor, the exhaust coughing wetly in the knee-high long-stemmed grass.

CHAPTER THREE

The plane goes over so low it puffs the leaves that shade the house. A high flowering privet hedge runs along the driveway, and right up until now he had liked the smell of privet. He still likes it, but he loves the clean smell of gas. At the end of the driveway there's a tilted barn, at the back of it an oil drum, propped on planks, then tipped so the gas drips from the spout. He can see the raindrop gleam of the drop that drips. Inside the barn old rubber tires hang on the hooks that were put up to store horse collars, the rafters at the back are stacked with empty five-gallon size oil cans. He can smell the bin of cobs, the corn molding in the sheller, the harness green as lichen on the walls, the barn itself tipped and damp as a sinkboard left to drain.

At the front of the house the clapboards are painted yellow to the height of a kitchen ladder. Another color, apple-green, is smeared in one thin coat on the frames of the windows. No path crosses the yard between the door and the mailbox because that is the front door and no one has used it. The house is a fine city house but it has learned to live out in the country. Except in illness, or death, no one is fool enough to use the front door to a farmhouse.

The sound in his ears is no longer that of the wind. He looks up to see bees swarming in the gable and the droning cloud that hovers over the house. The day is sultry. Much can hinge on a few drops of sweat. Warm spring rains have softened the driveway and the heels of his boots pull out with a slurp. He is experienced with dogs, but through the flowering privet he can see nothing but chickens in the lumpy backyard. The hens have scratched it into mounds and pits, marbled with dung. Jubal has been told that if you let your chickens run they will eat their own droppings and lay spotted eggs. His mother's chickens do not lay spotted eggs, but when stewed with dumplings they smell mighty funny. They lay their good eggs where nobody can find them until they hatch.

A chicken scratching in the drive scoots through the hedge and ducks under a corner of the back porch. This porch has no roof, and a woman sits there with her hair fanned out on her white shoulders. Is it all she wears? He can see the creamy whiteness of her back. She has just washed her hair; it is white at the tips, but still dark at the roots where her scalp gleams white. She sits in a rocker without arms, and her lap is full of apples and apple peelings. An enamel pail full of cored and peeled apples sits at her side. He can hear the sound when she cores an apple, and he can smell the fragrant scent of the peels. They lie around her like scrolls, already darkening. The cored apples in the pail are the color of bark. The woman wears no blouse, her white shoulders seem boneless, and he thinks of a basket of peeled ripe fruit. When she stoops for an apple her breasts spread on her lap like a woman's bottom. She is a soft white mound of female flesh. She peels the apples like his mother, round and round slowly, letting the string of the peel dangle, curling like a worm, until it falls in the furrow between her breasts. When it does she feels the coolness of it, dips a finger in the furrow to fish it out. The apple-scented tips of her fingers she then holds to her nose. Without a warning or a movement of her head she says, "Sanford?"

If he speaks will she holler? He is afraid to speak, or make a move to leave. "Sanford?" she repeats. Is it Jubal she smells or the apple? "*San-ford*," she says again, then turns to look at him with her serene unseeing eyes.

At the south edge of Pickett a bridge crosses the creek that both ornaments and often floods the college campus. In crossing it Hodler notes that the water runs high, and remembers that more rain is expected. It has been a wet spring. One day it is cold, the next it blows hot. This warm May morning nectar-drunken bees thump Hodler's windshield and he cranks the car window up to keep them out of his lap. The breeze is almost sultry. The smell of privet is like hot bread. The narrow blacktop road he follows is elm-lined and shaded, so that shadows half-conceal the small car in the ditch. That is not easy since the car is bright red, and tipped so the sky is reflected in the windshield. This flaming color is one of the owner's little jokes. It is as close as Felix Haffner can get to the luminous vibrant sox worn by teenagers. But it is not funny to Hodler that Haffner, a Jew, whose life was perverted by Nazi persecution, should go all the way to Munich to buy himself a Chinese-red Volkswagen, *cut-rate*.

But it is to Haffner. It is one of his characteristic coups. Hodler does not make too much of this, however, since he goes himself to a German dentist, who will use in his mouth only the best German-made drills. These too, and free of import duties, he brings back from the Homeland in vitamin capsules. It is a torment to Hodler to be told all of this, and while under novocain know he is a collaborator. The fact that some of the pain still comes through to him eases his guilt.

Hodler has been told that Haffner is *high* camp, but not knowing what low camp is little good it does him. This Haffner wears a beret, mouse-colored spats, shirts with detachable celluloid collars, a muffler so long the tassels threaten to trip him. No matter *what* drill is in his mouth, he feels no pain. Nevertheless Hodler likes him. Haffner is mad but unique. Dimly and with embarrassment Hodler senses that this queer, childish creature, impudent and half-crazy, has something more on the ball than himself. A fireman's red Volkswagen is merely one of his ways of pointing it up.

It does not surprise Hodler in the least to find this pram-size car tilted in the ditch weeds. Nor the windows cranked *down*, just in case it should rain. The keys will be found in the ignition. It is idle to warn Haffner on this subject, since he must either leave them there or spend his life looking for them. In his youth Haffner strolled in the Wiener Wald, which he often confuses with the woods around Pickett. If possessed by the need for a walk he will park the car, no matter where, and take one. These are all childish traits, and one could do worse than simply admit that Haffner is childish. But that, of course, explains nothing. A man is transparent. The child, bless its heart, is a mystery.

Hodler hastens to the scene of a crime or he would at least stop and crank up Haffner's windows. If the car is still there, he will do it on his way back. The news report at ten o'clock predicted more rain. The soft blacktop road shows a few fresh skid marks—but that, too, is not unusual. Haffner proceeds forward by jerks and hops: he stops by skids. It is the back end of the Volkswagen that shows all the wear. Thumps, dents, broad whacks, but above all, pushes. He has been pushed all the way from Cleveland. He has been pushed *to* Terre Haute. Hodler proceeds, distracted by Haffner, to where he sees Sanford Avery at the top of his driveway. It occurs to Hodler that the childish Haffner, seeing Avery waiting, would whoosh right on by him. In his rearview mirror he would see him bawl, flail his long arms. There is something about Avery that arouses such an impulse. Hodler, too, feels it. But he is not at all crazy. He even thinks he knows what is wrong with Avery. He is growing old. He has the jerky movements. He has the hoarse, baying voice. He fancies some people are laughing at him, and he is right. He wears a leisure-world cap with a ventilated crown, the long soiled bill with a red underlining. He has the stance of a peasant carving weighted to stand upright. Seen from the side Avery resembles something swallowed by a monstrous bird, and regurgitated. The red flannel bill lining gives the lie of health to his sallow face. A heavy cotton flannel shirt pads out his narrow shoulders and puffs out the seat of his khaki pants. There is room for a child to stand between his flexed bowed legs. He wags one hand, then lets it fall with a slap on the mailbox that stands high as his shoulder, mounted on a post that is sunk in a milk can weighted with sand. To relax him Hodler says: "That's some mailbox, Avery."

"Didn't come with the place," Avery replies, which means that Avery supplied it. In his spare time Avery turns out products people urge him to patent, but that takes money. One is a cuspidor with a removable disposable lining, an idea both somewhat ahead of and behind its time. Another, which he produces on order, is a shoe-salesman's stool provided with a mirror so the customer can see, without rising, how the merchandise looks to everybody else. This stool can also be used for shining shoes, or diverting children who are waiting for a haircut. One can be seen at the front of the Pickett Fire Station all summer long.

Hodler makes a move to park in the driveway, but Avery shoos him away, flagging both arms. There is something in the driveway. He beckons Hodler to come and look. Where the earth is softened by rain Avery stoops to point at the tracks. The tread marks form a crisp diamond pattern, but Hodler finds them small. "A bike?" he says.

Avery snorts as if blowing under a shower. The way people can't see what's right beneath their nose is a torment to him.

"Motorbike," he says, "one of them goddam snorters!"

Crossing over this track is the one made by Avery with the snow tires on his Ford pickup. He stoops and points, "See here?" Hodler stoops to see the heel holes punched into the grass edging the drive. "Went along here to keep from crunchin' in the gravel." Hodler exchanges a glance with Sherlock Holmes Avery. It may be a rape for Miss Holly, but for Avery it's a scoop.

"How is she?" says Hodler, peering down the driveway. Avery's pickup sets in the garage, a battered power mower roped to the cab. The air still smells of the exhaust. The cooling metal cracks. Avery sets himself to say, "Who in the hell would know that!" but something reminds him that he has already said it, several times.

"Mussed up," he says, "he really mussed her up."

Hodler turns to avoid looking at him. He senses that Avery is crammed to the brim with newsworthy details. Through the hedge Hodler sees the shabby, run-down yard, the earth chicken-pitted, the weedy fringes cluttered with junk, berry boxes, and rusty farm machinery, the very picture of serenity, languor and peace associated with rural dilapidation. Under a tree dying at the top, a buggy seat was bird-splattered and stained with mulberries. It tipped as if Burl Ives sat there, plucking a string.

Nothing seemed further removed from crime, from the headlines of violence.

"This bastard's smart," says Avery, "he had it all worked out. Wouldn't you think he'd been a little neater about it?" What does he mean by that? Hodler would rather not ask. "He had it all worked out," Avery says, "but he couldn't take a minute just to rinse his hands off. Can you beat that?"

Hodler can't. He goes off down the drive.

"He couldn't take the time, I guess," says Avery. "Then, I guess, I come along and surprised him. All he could do was git."

Hodler walks to where a footpath breaks the hedge and crosses the drive to a sagging privy. The door is around at the back, facing a meadow where several black Swiss cows are grazing. A wonderful place to sit. A smart-enough criminal might be sitting there.

"He comes along here," says Avery, "you can see his tracks. Then, he sees her on the porch here, he sees her peelin' apples. She'd just washed her hair. Half her clothes were off."

It is curious how clearly Hodler sees it. The woman seated on the chair, a platform rocker, her blond, wheat-colored hair fanned out on her shoulders, her corset loosened, the cloud of hovering bees and the knife curling the peel of apple. Her back would have been to the man in the driveway, so he might have stood here for some time, watching. That was when it really happened. While he stood here watching his lust built up. Hodler blinks his eyes and listens to the drone of the bees.

"Left her sittin' here," says Avery, "just a towel around her shoulders. I was gone a little better than forty minutes. In the time I was gone she peeled a couple dozen apples and got herself raped."

Hodler notes that bits of peel are strewn about the porch, and that the apples in the pail are now rust-colored. Bees and flies crawl on them. It is the scent of the drying peels that he smells.

"Way I see it," says Avery, "he come up behind her. Thought he would surprise her comin' up behind her, but she had this knife in her hand, and she give him a slash. When he tried to get it away he either cut her, or she cut herself. She's got a cut on her thumb."

In the trees along the driveway several grackles are squawking; one dives at Avery's head. He stoops, scoops up a handful of gravel, then wheels and throws it skyward like a small boy. It rains on the hood of the car and the roof of the barn. "Goddam birds," he says, and parts the hedge so that Hodler can step into the yard. Screened on one side, roofless, the porch opens on the yard like a stage. Everything is still on it but the actors. Miss Holly's platform rocker occupies the front and center, the green velvet seat like a cushion without pins. To make it low enough for her it has no casters. Strewn around it on three sides are apple peelings. Bees crawl on the quartered slices in the pan. A paring knife with a bleached wooden handle lies where Miss Holly dropped it. The blade is sticky with juice and tipped with dried blood. Where the porch is bare both bees and apple peelings have been crushed. It is shameful how clearly Hodler sees it all: a sweaty, grunting wrestle scented with apples. No screams or cries for help. Just the drone of the bees. Hodler would like to know if she had been stung. The porch is raised above the yard and in the dust beneath it, heaped in mounds by the chickens, there is a leghorn egg, white as milk glass.

"That wasn't there," says Avery, and stoops to pick it up, leaving the scene exactly as he found it. He scrapes his thumbnail on the shell of the egg, an annoying sound. "Found her lyin' there," he says, pointing with the egg, "bloomers torn half off, rip in her corset. Otherwise you might have thought she was nappin'."

Hodler sees it all through the rapist's eyes. He blinks, says, "She was unconscious?"

"No more than per usual. Had her eyes wide open."

Hodler has the curious feeling they have both rehearsed it. Avery has the answers, Hodler the questions.

"Except for Holly," he says, "it's just as I found it. Except for her and the egg."

Hodler says, "Hmmm."

"He mussed her up all right. Tore her corset half off. But the funny thing is why he got her so dirty—"

"It's not exactly a friendly little tussle, is it Avery? If she put up a scrap he'd be bound to get her dirty—"

"Don't mean that," says Avery. "It's *where* he got her dirty. She's not dirty at all except where he bit her. Like to bit her tit off."

Hodler does not wince, but he flinches. His eyes blink. The word tit is three letters, not four, but it gives Hodler even more trouble. Part of the pleasure Avery feels in this rehearsal is to see it on the face of Hodler.

55

"Like to bit it off," he says, "but that's not so unusual. Guess these perverts have to bite somethin'. Funny thing is why he got her so dirty. Got her titty all smeared."

"A man intent on rape," says Hodler, "doesn't often take the time to wash his hands."

"This one didn't," says Avery. "Nor his face either. How'd this pervert get himself so dirty?"

Hodler says, "Avery, I know how you feel. But it's not going to help to call him a pervert."

"No?" he says. "You should see it. Bit into her like he would a goddam apple! Like to bit it off!" The egg Avery holds he tosses into the air, catches. A rose-tinted sweat shines on his face. Hodler has never seen him so animated. In the sultry bee-drone Hodler sees sprouting from the head of Avery the horns of the satyr. In his face no changes are necessary, he has the ear-to-ear leer. Shamelessly he dips a hand into his pocket, digs at his crotch. Nor can Hodler, a hand to his eyes, screen off the picture of Miss Holly, sprawled among the apples, offering the apple-colored nipple of her ample breast. "See that knife?" says Avery. "By god, she nicked him. If she didn't fight him off she managed to slash him! That's his blood on the knife."

"He leave anything else?" Hodler is relieved that no cuts show on Avery.

"How about teeth marks?" Avery says. "Must be fingerprints all over her ass."

From the pail of unpeeled apples Hodler takes one, buffs it on his shirt sleeve. He is a prudent man, slow to panic, skeptical of current fads and fashions, but it is clear that Sanford Avery suffers from a crime he failed to commit.

"She see him?" says Hodler.

"She see *what?*"

"Think she'd recognize him if she saw him?"

Avery wags his head as he whinnies. "Recognize him? Know what he looks like, Hodler?" Is it like *Hodler?* That is how Avery grins. "You won't believe it. Says he looks like a spaceman. How you like that?"

"A what?"

"Spaceman," says Avery. "She sees them on the TV. Thinks she was humped by a goddam spaceman. How you like that?"

Hodler makes no comment. He seems to be wondering.

"You don't believe it?"

Oh yes, he believes it. If that's what she said, he can believe it. If that's what she saw he can almost see it himself. The monster with the goggles, the astronaut helmet, coming out of nowhere with the snort of a rocket. Avery squints at the sky as if he might see him up there. The rocket noise is there and seems to be approaching. A small, rocking plane, spraying the neighboring orchard, goes over them so low the shadow flicks them. Avery thrusts his fist up, shakes it. "The sunuvabitch, I wouldn't put it past him!" The spray falls like a drizzle on Avery's upturned face.

Hodler has taken off his glasses to buff the lenses with his tie. Avery has stooped to shoo the flies from the pan of quartered apples, plop a quarter into his mouth. "How is she?" Hodler says.

Not to disturb the scene of the crime they go back along the side of the house to the front. Avery, out of long habit, scrapes his shoes on the doormat. There is no stoop nor porch. It is known that Mrs. Stohrmeyer picked a house without one just to keep Miss Holly out of sight from the road. The only porch is at the back. A bay window just out to the left of the door, and through the faded lace curtain Hodler sees a hooded bird cage, the material so thin he sees the two birds on the perch. So does Avery. The cage rocks when he steps inside and jerks off the cloth. The startled lovebirds rock like toys. "I can't do everything," says Avery, and uses the towel to dust the shade of the lamp. His shoes leave tracks in the dust on the floor. "Fellow from Terre Haute," says Avery, dusting out the cloth, "says he'll buy anything we'd like to sell." What would it be? He speaks with more wonderment than pride. Hodler stares at the volumes in a glass-covered case and recalls that Mrs. Stohrmeyer was a wild-flower expert. The country house is jammed with her city furniture, sheets drape the upholstered chairs. Near the stairs is a Gramophone, with the lid up, sheet music piled on the shelf beneath it. Above it hangs an Audubon print of a bird attacking a snake. Avery leans forward to level the frame, flick the dust cloth at the brass balls on the andirons. Hodler stands with his hand on the banister rail, facing the door beneath the stairs. The door is ajar, a table covered with oilcloth reflects the glare of light at the window where a man has cupped his hands to his face to light a cigarette. He wears a broad-brimmed Western hat. A cloud of swirling smoke conceals his face. Hodler lifts his hand to silence Avery, but his own mouth goes dry and he cannot speak. The man at the window smokes, a sensuous smile of satisfaction on his weathered face. The illusion is so perfect Hodler listens for his cough, the sound of his lips. Then, flick, he is gone, and the sun-filled window frames a pack of cigarettes with filter tips. The pack pops open, the cigarettes pop up. At Hodler's elbow Avery says, "Guess she left the sound off. She likes to watch movies with the sound off. How you figure that?" The movie with the sound off returns to the screen: a helicopter hovers above a small boat tossed by soundless waves. "This way," says Avery, and gives the banister rail a dusting as he goes up the stairs to the landing. The bathroom door stands open, and Avery steps in to jiggle the knob on the john, tighten a dripping faucet nozzle. You can't do everything, he repeats, and does everything that needs to be done. Hodler waits while he opens the screen at the window, shoos out the flies. He waits while Avery dampens a washrag at the spigot, then goes down the hall with it to a door at the end, which he opens without knocking. He waits while Avery steps in, leaving the door ajar, then steps out and beckons to him. "This way," he says.

In the room Hodler enters the shades are drawn. He sees nothing but the flare of light around their edges. A bulb that hangs from the ceiling comes on, goes off, then comes on and stays when Avery twists it in the socket. It glows so feebly, however, Hodler can gaze at the luminous twist of wire. Directly beneath it is a bed, and the woman seated on it lifts her hands as if to reach for something, or ward something off. Hodler sees the gleaming part in her hair and the small hand up with the thumb extended. The fleshy part of the thumb is split by a cut, and is like a small penis gripped by a child. The cut is fresh and moist. She has been sitting there sucking it.

"It's me, Holly," says Avery. "It's me and Mr. Hodler."

Her eyes reflect the bulb like a piece of gold wire. She looks from Avery to Hodler, back to Avery, then returns the thumb to her mouth, like a cork. Avery gropes for the hand, finds it, presses the thumb down flat, lowers the hand to her lap. "There now," he says, and pats it. She looks inert and heavy. A creamy mound of female flesh. Her breasts have spilled into her lap, and Hodler wonders how he ever got her up here. Matter-of-factly Avery says, "Don't suck it, Holly. Just hold it."

In the same tone she says, "I cut it."

"Sure," he says, "you cut it." He stoops as if to look at it. "See here," he says. In the flare of a match Hodler can't help but see. He turns away, but too late. The lobbing breast of Miss Holly, the colors of a healing bruise, has a nipple like a bite in a russet apple. In it, but not out of it. The bite has left marks like a trap's teeth. Hodler has fixed his eyes on the light bulb as the match sputters out.

60

"Some spaceman, eh?" says Avery, and whinnies.

Hodler finds it hard to put his mind to it. In this feeble yellow light, like that in a manger, Miss Holly seems to crouch with a nursing baby. Her scalp glistens where the hair is parted. The scent that rises from her body is that of soap and apples.

"A space-man," she says.

"Some joke!" says Avery. "Why'd he get her so dirty? Dirt all over one titty. How you figure that?"

Hodler notes that the walls, all around, are hung with pictures: calendar pictures of babies, pictures of laughing, happy children, pictures of lambs, and kittens, pictures of religious subjects. Christ on the Cross, Christ rising from the Dead, Christ healing the sick, Noah building the Ark, God speaking to Moses out of the whirlwind. Was a spaceman so unusual? Only in his more abandoned, passionate moments. Like ordinary mortals he was pressed for time. He didn't have it to spare to wash his face, or his hands.

Hodler says, "She's been assaulted, Avery. You sure she's been raped?"

"Some joke!" says Avery. "How the hell'd I know that?"

Hodler is grateful for the room's dim light. Miss Holly watches him with interest. Does he remind her of the spaceman? Does she wonder what they might do next?

"Before you let it out," says Hodler, "you ought to be sure about it."

"And how can I be sure without lettin' it out?" He

whinnies loudly, then says, "You want to know somethin', Hodler. What if she's right?"

On his mind's eye Hodler sees the headlines—

VISITING SPACEMAN

ASSAULTS

HOLLY STOHRMEYER

He does not say, some joke. Miss Holly sits quietly, clothed in her wheat-colored hair, a woman patiently awaiting further visitations. Was it perhaps like the first time a woman was taken? The caveman, too, might have been a hasty lover, with a dirt-smeared face.

"She knows what's what more'n you think," says Avery. "Now she knows what it's like, which is more'n some women."

"I don't doubt that," says Hodler.

"So she thinks he's a spaceman, eh? Is that so dumb?"

Hodler turns his back to the light, squints to look at his watch. "Ten after eleven. I got to get back."

"She's cooked if I let it out," says Avery, "maybe I'm cooked if I don't. Say he knocked her up?"

It is not like Hodler to banter, but he says, "A spacenik, Avery. What'll you name it?"

It is Avery who sweats, but he stoops to wipe her face with the washrag. "You hungry?" he asks. She shakes her head. "Then stop suckin' that thumb, you hear me? You'll suck it off." He places her hand once more in her lap, then stands erect to twist the bulb loose in the socket. It makes little difference in the light. Avery follows

Hodler into the hall, then goes ahead of him to the bath-room. The door stands open while he pees.

"What'll we do?" he says.

"Report it quick," says Hodler.

"I did," says Avery. "First thing I did was report it to you."

He goes ahead of Hodler on the stairs, and gives the screen at the front a kick to pop it open. It has no spring on it and swings wide to flap on the house. Knees flexed, to go easy on the grass, Avery pads ahead of Hodler across the weedy lawn to the road. The sun-warmed air is a cloud of buzzing gnats. Hodler fans his hat at them, but they stick to his hands, the perspiration on his forehead. They get in between his glasses and his eyes, and he thumps into Avery who has stooped in the driveway.

"We got teeth prints, ass prints, tire prints," he says. "We got the works." Is it a grin Hodler sees on his face, or a squint? His teeth are like the last kernels on a dried cob. What impression would they leave on a woman's breast? It occurs to Hodler that the evil men do is less depressing than their vagrant, idle thoughts. In the hot cab of his car he cranks the window down, gulps for air. He says, "I must say she's taking it pretty well."

"She's not so bad off," says Avery. "I know women who are worse off." He gives Hodler a dilated, comical, leering wink. The pleated webbing around one eye crin-kles: his face requires a moment to return to normal. "She's not so bad off, you know. She's free to think what she thinks. You and me can sit and think our ass off, Hodler, but it won't get us a fat spacelady."

Hodler is too startled to be sure of what he hears. "I got to run," he says, but it was not his intention to come down the way he did on the gas pedal. The wheels spin. The gravel scatters to fall in the milk can, ping on the mailbox. Hodler wears no space helmet, but one might think that he had just been shot into orbit. The motor snorts. A blue plume of exhaust covers his tracks. He is hardly like a Moslem prayer-borne toward Mecca, but what he does, however awkwardly, comes natural. He is just naturally awkward. He burns more rubber than gasoline. He comes riding to where the blacktop narrows and there is a color in the ditch like a fire burning. That is Haffner's Volkswagen. Showers are forecast and both the windows are down. Any other car would have been the owner's business, but Haffner's is everybody's business, especially when it is bad. Hodler slams on his brakes—he leaves skid marks that will later confuse and confound Sheriff Cantrill—then he parks in some shade, leaving his own windows down, and walks back to crank up those of Haffner. The humidity is bad. Hodler is wet both inside and out. Birds seem to swim in the brothy air, solid objects to float. Nevertheless, Hodler is puzzled to see the clouds vibrating in the car's insect-spattered windshield. Neither the road nor the sky shimmers with heat. Moving closer he sniffs the car's exhaust and realizes that the motor is still running. That is not unusual. No, that too is par for the Haffner course. If asked, he will tell you it is how he keeps charged the battery. The blue exhaust stirs the long-stemmed grass when the motor coughs. Hodler is so hot and mad he comes up fast and yanks the door on the driver's side open. The man slouched there, collapsed, almost spills into his lap. Is it Haffner? A brown paper bag has been placed on his head, then squashed. When Hodler tips it back crushed black cherries spill into Haffner's lap, the juice streams down his face. But it is Haffner. No other face has such a nose. Is it cherry juice or blood that drips from its tip? There is also a lump behind one ear, but that just might be Haffner. Is he alive? He is alive if one is not too particular. The breath of life stirs the hairs in his nose and dries the blood-red juice on his lips.

Hodler leaves the bag on him, fearing something worse, and props him gently in the opposite corner. Bees crawl on his hands and cluster to the stains on his front. Hodler slips behind the steering wheel, which proves to be sticky, and grips the knob of the gearshift. But when he lets out the clutch the motor balks, dies. Some time passes before it will start. Understandably, Hodler is a little nervous, and when the motor does start the car leaps forward. Haffner's banged nose is banged again, and a puff of wind carries off the paper bag. The sight is gory. He appears to have been crowned with a cherry pie. His head lolls on the car door where the breeze revives him: the wind narrows his juice-stained, bloodshot eyes. Are they on Hodler? He can't bear to look. Aloud he says, "Haffner, what happened?"

Haffner has been pondering just that question. That's what he was doing when Hodler found him. He is doing it now. "You woot nod bleef it!" he says. There is pride in his voice. But for once he has underestimated Hodler.

"I believe it," says Hodler. "A spaceman."

Hodler does not wish him dead, not for a moment, but it is a special pleasure to find Haffner speechless. His frizzly hair is a tangle of pits and crushed cherries, behind the smear on his face no particular expression. The bird-like eyes are steady, an aging bacchic imp crowned with freshly trod grapes. From Pickett, siren whining, the Sheriff's car goes by with a puffing whoosh. The wail of the siren lingers; as it fades Hodler says, "You left your motor running again, you know that? One day you're going to get a ticket for it."

Haffner makes no comment. There are many to be made, but he keeps his peace. He is smart enough to know that this is Hodler's hour. He rides with his chin on the door, a well-bred pooch with a lust for travel. Hodler drives him into Pickett, where the wind is rising, and the historic elm on the corner has fallen. A crowd has gathered to watch it be sawed into souvenirs. At another time Hodler, as well as Haffner, would appreciate the sentiments of such a moment, but the wind is rising, and the day, so to speak, has just begun. Already more has fallen than an historic elm. Haffner appears to doze as Hodler drives him through the yellow blinker at the intersection, the wind like the hot exhaust from the rasping saw. At the emergency entrance to the clinic an ice cream truck is unloading bags of ice cubes. The driver and the nurse have taken time out to suck on pieces of ice. Hodler waits, the motor idling, but the ice is slow to melt. He toots the horn, cries, "This man needs attention!" He has to make himself heard above the crunch of the ice.

"I can see that," the nurse replies. "What's his name?"

She stands with her pad on its clipboard, waiting. The tip of the ball-point pen she taps on the pad. "Will you give me his name?"

Who would believe that Hodler cannot recall it? Of all men, perhaps only Haffner. His mind is a blank. Has he lost it? The nurse bends down to look at the victim, his head lolls loosely to the car's vibration.

"Isn't that Dr. Haffner?" she says, and moves to get a little more of the profile. Dr. Haffner it is. More hawk-like than ever with the swelling nose.

"Whatever happened?"

"Miss——" Hodler begins, but Haffner interrupts him.

"A spaze-mann!" he says, and smiles a thin smile. His eyes remain sealed. Without glancing at Hodler the nurse writes on her pad, "*Haffner, Felix, Pickett College.*"

"And *your* name?" she says.

CHAPTER FOUR

Ma'am—" he says, "I'm not Sanford."

The face she turns toward him has a bit of the apple peel at her lips. It is round as a child's, pretty as a child's, with a child's unblinking, wide-eyed gaze. The pupils dilate as if a light had flashed in her face. The fingers she has just sniffed pass before her eyes in a gentle, absent-minded gesture, lightly combing her forehead, as if for loose strands of hair. She makes no sound. He wonders if the pale, water-blue eyes might be blind. "Ma'am—" he repeats, and takes a step toward her, as if to move into her focus. She lowers her gaze to look, with astonishment, at her thumb. She has cut herself. The soft fleshy part of it streams with blood. A moment she stares at it, front and side, then she suddenly thrusts it, like a gift, toward Jubal. It is like a child's penis. Can he help it if that's what it is like? Like a child she thrusts it toward him to make it well, perhaps, or kiss it. "You cut it, Ma'am—" he says, and moves to take a look at it. She gives the small hand to him, the thumb and palm bloody and sticky and he does what he would do to a thumb of his own: he gives it a suck. "There now—" he says as he would to a child, but the hand pulls away from him as she keels over, the apples spill from her lap and roll on the porch. He has to grab her to keep her from falling, her head lolls on his arm. He is on his knees, the weight of her body rests on his thighs, one of his hands grips her shoulder, and it is no fault of his if so much of her spills from the corset. Her head lolls back so he can see the bits of apple in her open mouth. He makes an effort to hoist her, taking her by the loose arm, like a dancer, but it is easier to let her sprawl out like spilled milk. There she lies on a bed of apples, scented with the peels. Some there are, no doubt, who do not dream of taking an overripe beauty where she lies sleeping, her hair, her stays, and all her defenses down. He is not one of them. But his experience has been with a woman who fights him, and it is easier, strangely enough, to take a woman who wrestles and fights you than a woman who sprawls out like spilled milk, her body inert. He tries to help himself sensibly, without panic, kneeling to straddle her like a cushion, but he doesn't like trying to take a woman on a porch without a roof, in a chicken-littered yard. He likes the idea of cover. If he can't have cover he likes it dark. He has the best of intentions, but without experience he is like a greenhorn on a bucking bronco; he grabs what he can, closes his eyes, and holds on tight. He has the impression that his head is severed from a tail that wags and thrusts. He sows the furrow as he plows it, a gag in his mouth. Nevertheless, at the height of his panic he hears the sound of brakes out on the highway, the spray of gravel as the wheels twist into the drive. His severed tail goes on wagging but his head is up, like a calf from a milk pail, an accurate enough description if the calf can be imagined with the pail on its head. That is how it would look to anyone coming down the drive. The helmet is like a white bowl or pail clamped on the head of an animal running for cover. He goes on all fours, scattering the startled chickens, to where a wire croquet loop trips him sprawling; then he goes through the barn, like a tunnel of darkness, into the orchard that lies behind it, the trees so low he has to run without looking up. Behind him he leaves the cough of an idling motor, the cackle and squawk of the startled hens, and a woman who knows as little as he does just what it is that has happened. She lies on her back, her ample charms exposed and strewn with discolored apple peelings, flies crawl on her finger, which has stopped bleeding, bees crawl on the moist, blackened teat of one breast. Apples that have been crushed, and peelings that have been rubbed, give off a fragrant, bee-clouded scent. A pullet pecks at the piece of crushed peel between her bloomer'd knees. The man who stands there cannot believe his eyes. Several times he hoarsely shouts the word *Holly* at her, then he stoops, one hand braced on his knee, to put a soiled brown finger to the black smear on her breast. Her eyes are open, but it is a moment before she smiles.

"Holly!" he says. "It's me. You hear me?"

One never knows. That is one of his problems.

"You hear me!" he shouts. "What happened?"

She lies gazing at the sky above her, her eyes as blue as that sky and as bottomless. From the pail he takes a slice of a quartered apple and snorfels as he eats it. "What happened?" he repeats, knowing he will never know, and looks at the paring knife she is holding. Flies crawl on the sticky blade and the cut on her thumb. Still erect, the bruised nipple of her breast is like a valve from which the air escaped from a bladder. He is tempted to moisten it with spittle, see where it leaks.

"You cut yourself," he says, matter-of-factly, and helps himself to another slice of the apple, as strangely discolored as the overripe fruit of her breast.

Under cover of the plane's roar Jubal pushes the bike to where the weeds grow tall at the rear of the pump house. The question is no longer which way to run, but which way to walk. His inclination is downgrade, where the road is in shadow, because the duffle is heavy and his sore knees tremble, but looking down there he sees the mirror'd reflection of the sun on an approaching car windshield. When this car comes up behind him he is headed upgrade, the guitar at his back. The car comes up fast, then slows to go around him: the rear lights blink on as it brakes to a stop. He hears the horn toot, he sees the hand wave as if beckoning. Jubal runs toward it, swinging his duffle, to put his head in the window opposite the driver. The man behind the wheel is no larger than a child, and looks to Jubal like a clever Hollywood chimp, trained to drive a car. He nods and smiles with a blood-red stain on his teeth and lips. In his lap, the top open, he holds a brown paper bag, which he hoists in the air and gives a shake, like a rattle. Then he thrusts it toward Jubal whose head is framed in the door. The bag contains black cherries, and the stems of cherries. He shakes it at Jubal. What does he want him to do? He cannot speak because of how he laughs. Out toward Jubal he thrusts the paper bag. But his eyes are creased, his head wags from side to side as he laughs. What is so funny? As he laughs now, he chokes. Bits of chewed skin and cherry pits spit in his lap. He can't stop laughing. He can't stop shaking the bag in Jubal's face. So Jubal takes it, spreads wide the top, then without opening the door he leans far over and plops it, like a paper hat, on the wagging head. He holds it there: he squishes it around as if he was squeezing the juice from an orange. Does that stop him? No, if anything it is worse. He has doubled over laughing. He will either laugh or choke to death. Juice from the squashed cherries streams down his face. In his irritation Jubal sort of thumps him, leaving the pewter-colored smear of one knuckle on him, but little effect it has. He chokes and gasps. Jubal thinks to go around him and give him a shake, but when he leans from the window the car starts moving. It hops, then balks. It settles down to a balky, halting, coast. Jubal trots along behind it, he hollers *Hey there! Hey!*, at one point his hand rests on it, as if he means to push it, and so they go along to where high ditch weeds, and several inches of water, bring the car to a stop. The motor continues to idle and he can hear the wet cough of the exhaust.

Bees were feeding on pits and skins of the cherries when Jubal waded to peer through the windshield: the vibration of the motor made the man's head wiggle as if he still laughed. Jubal is no fool, he knows people are strange, but he hadn't really believed they were crazy. He thinks about splashing some of the ditch water on him, but up the road, from the north, another car is approaching. Fenced in by the rain-soft ditches he runs for the bridge. Up ahead a sign tells him he is entering Pickett, an unincorporated town with nine houses of worship, one liberal arts college, and one Army & Navy Surplus Outlet. At this time in the morning a rippled sheet of green plastic keeps the sun off the display of merchandise in the window, and casts a shadow like an illness on the figure framed in the door.

▬

O. Kashperl (the O is for Oscar) stands in a draft that would blow a smaller man over. He watches two Pickett firemen, in rolled top boots, hose down the sidewalk in front of the firehouse, where, at the curbing, the Sheriff's car is illegally parked. The figure of Kashperl appears foreshortened, but that illusion is customary. If he stands near an object the scale seems off. In spite of the temperature, and the season, he wears a topcoat that hangs within inches of his shoes. The material is chinchilla, it was tailored in Odessa, home of Kashperl's dreams and the Moldavanka gangsters whose blood—and it drained them to do it—now flows in his veins. He wears the coat draped on his shoulders, the cuffs of the empty sleeves tucked into his pockets. The effect is that of a giant who stands at slightly parted folding doors. The empty sleeves suggest

73

the veteran amputee who blocks the steps of the post office, his cigarbox of shoelaces and poppies concealed by the flap of his unbuttoned coat.

Kashperl is not everybody's type, but he is a good tax accountant. With Hodler he is considered one of the three most eligible Pickett bachelors. The other is, or rather was, Felix Haffner, who is now considered more AC than DC. Mrs. Klett, a very DC widow, has recently shifted from Haffner to Kashperl, who loves her matzoh balls and schokolade tort smothered with schlag.

Is it surprising that a man like Kashperl deals in army and navy surplus, the clothes of men *missing in action* his specialty? A man with this sort of taste might prove to have unpredictable talents. As he has. Kashperl the impresario, the diviner of talent in others. Just before Christmas, in a Texaco oil pit, he stumbled on a graceless, acne'd dropout with the unlikely name of Rompers. His eyes were shifty. He looked unhealthy. How did Kashperl sense that teenage girls were swooning to sip this standing marsh water? Talent is talent. How does the swallow know the hour and the day at Capistrano?

This hour and this day, Kashperl takes a break to combat his caffeine-withdrawal headache. The withdrawal is in an instant. The replenishment takes twenty minutes to an hour. Anyone pressed for time, or for surplus pants, knows, however, just where to find him. The dark end of the Bickel drug and lunch counter is known to be his. There he stands, unable to squeeze between the stools that line the counter. Through the window, shaded by an awning, he observes the day's major event: the felling of an historic campus elm. Small fry stand in a circle anxious to be hit by falling branches. A rising wind sways the branch supporting the man with the saw. This elm is special. It is known to have been there when the Indians scalped the first settlers, hardy, stubborn men who worked like slaves to deprive their children of all simple pleasures, and most reasons to live.

Is it more than a tree that falls? It falls to give this day its meaning. To give Kashperl a cud for his idle, vagrant thoughts. Over the half-curtain at the window Kashperl has a panoramic view of the square. In the winter, packed with snow, it glares. In early May it is like a veiled dancer. Kashperl has actually said so, publicly. God knows what he means. All three of Mr. Bickel's board-flat, sallow daughters have heard, with their own wide ears, Kashperl's comment. Veiled women they are not. Would to God they were. These sweet sad girls are a worry to Kashperl, but his poetic gifts are wasted on them. All he can do is drink much Bickel coffee, and leave them large tips. They have no talent. Worse, they seem to have no dreams. The acne'd Rompers boy, brought here for coffee, preferred to look at his own sorry face in the mirror than let his narrow, shifty eyes flatter such girls.

The Bickel daughters lie, that is, outside of the Kashperl enterprises. Alike as old socks, wearing aprons soiled where their thighs and bellies rub against the counter, they stand with soft, folded arms watching Kashperl eat his jelly doughnut, hardly the food for a man who resembles nothing so much as a hog. Their worry is for him, the cream and sugar he takes in his daily eight to ten cups of coffee. Their worry is for a man so big he no longer seems to care.

Everything has its history. In a room with high windows, the radiators pounding, all the lights out but the one in the smoking lantern, a Miss Elvira Josephare acquainted Kashperl with the lineaments of art. It was Kashperl's duty, each Friday, to draw the blinds, get out the slides, and operate the magic lantern. Everybody in the class who had the brains they were born with used this period to sleep while the slides were showing. Everybody but Kashperl, who had more brains, weekly, and the lecturer who tapped on the screen with her pointer. In her left hand she gripped a dancer's castanets, which she clattered to indicate a slide change. The alternating rhythm of her voice and the clatter helped the smart ones to sleep. The hot windless room smelled of the lecturer's perfume and the bag of sachet she kept loose in her purse. She used it as a pitcher, in a crisis on the mound, stooped to finger the bag of resin. A Spanish shawl draped her shoulders, the tassels swaying when her freckled arm gestured with the pointer. In such wise did Kashperl also learn the lineaments of style. Nothing he later gazed upon in his travels proved as memorable as this cave of darkness, and Michelangelo's "David," or his "Pietà," projected upside down. When Kashperl at long last confronted these creations he secretly resented their right-side-upness. Kashperl could not paint, nor draw with charcoal, nor make out of clay acceptable ashtrays, his talent being that of the man whose twig bends in the presence of water. Kashperl the diviner. Is it so important how he looks? A nameless college instructor put it more bluntly: "Kewpy," he said, "you have a syrup but it doesn't pour."

The pain this caused Kashperl was small compared to his pleasure in knowing the source of this comment was Gertrude Stein. It is a talent to know a good thing when you see it, and to suffer it.

Kashperl's preference for things anonymous and faceless, for things that have been waiting, so to speak, for Kashperl, led him to examine precisely those objects other people inclined to throw away. Prints without signatures, books without titles or authors, left the shock of recognition up to Kashperl. The exercise of this taste became his talent: Kashperl became the collaborator. A preference for the fading title, or the missing author, or better yet the rare volume that proved to lack both, a country waiting to be staked out and mapped by Kashperl. What began as an unusual hobby soon enough became an addiction. But that is not unusual. Men are either addicts or peddlers. That too is a coinage Kashperl purloined from the sepia pages of a nameless book. It is this that persuades the syrup of Kashperl to pour. Otherwise he would merely be another squirrel hoarding his loot in a windowless bedroom, the windows covered over to make room for shelves. Something more than three thousand volumes line the walls. There they all are, in neatly kept rows, but not one of these volumes has a visible author on the spine. A few have numbers, applied by Kashperl in a moment of weakness, a hunger for order, but this soon passed. He likes the disorder better. The play of chance. When he takes down a book who knows what he might find?

Time, circumstance, and even Kashperl have changed. It is not the same book he glanced at in the past, any more than his friends are the same people. But his friends have labels, they play roles, and they think they have been discovered. The shock—and it is a shock—is of familiarity. To see in a face no more, and no less, than what one knows.

Time was when a man opened his Bible at random and glanced down the page for the orphic statement, the mirrored truth, that the circumstance seemed to call for. Time was, and for Kashperl this time still is. He finds it when he turns to an anonymous book, or fixes his gaze on a nameless face. He must interpret the writing on the wall, or the page, or the face, by himself. That detail is important. He must find it, not be told it.

We might say that all these nameless, anonymous objects were suffering from amnesia until Kashperl's coming. He brings the shock of recognition. He claims to know who they really are. This might be just a highborn way of making forgery pay, but whatever it is, it is Kashperl. He lives on it and by it. The mania comes to him naturally. On those tilted, weighted carts out in front of used-book stores, or tables strewn with salvage, or the carts in supermarkets, the seeing-eye of Kashperl recognizes the anonymous article of value. Or so he believes. The cart of cans without labels, knocked down in price and dented, waiting for the bargain hunter or the idle gambler, is for Kashperl an object of mystical properties. So is the stranger who makes an unheralded appearance in the wings of Kashperl's life. Such a stranger comes toward him, his helmet gleaming, swinging what else but a surplus army duffle, and wearing what else but a pair of Kashperl's cut-rate boots on his feet. He walks, but it is clear from his awkward gait he is accustomed to ride.

Another man might find this walk mighty peculiar, but not Kashperl. It is the gait of a greenhorn in stirrup heel boots. Both the boots and the pants, with their ass-tight pockets, are current best-sellers at the Army Surplus. So is the helmet with the amber-hued visor, an astro-nut on the Bob Hope program. So is the jacket that he wears unzipped to expose the portrait of J. S. Bach. Best-sellers all, but here in Pickett, Brahms edges Bach, thanks to his beard. Kashperl also might have sold him the green army duffle that swings on its cord to sweep the grass, and the guitar, in the plastic case, that hangs at his back. Kashperl could do worse than hire this boy to sit in his window or stand in front at the curbing. Everything is familiar, in stock, and selling—except the face. The spattered visor conceals it, but Kashperl knows the type. Lumpy pimples on the shoulders, bad teeth, advanced athlete's feet. So well does Kashperl know him he can smell the ointment on what will prove to be his duck's ass hairdo, taste the smoke from his helmet-crushed cigarette. In this or any other life a very dusty answer, but Kashperl watches him like a sunning lizard. Is he comical or frightening? Where did he leave his gas-eating mount? He comes along the curbwalk, his ankles rocking, to where he finds a meter with some free time on it. That is important. He gives it a hard slap with the heel of his hand. Then he stoops to open the top of his duffle, dip his hand to the elbow, scrounge around in the contents. What is it he has? A length of cable with loops at both ends. The duffle and the guitar he props against the meter post, loops the cable around them, padlocks the looped ends. With a gesture the meter is now a grave marker. Does it tick off the time before the dead will arise? In Kashperl's book this is style, and he is impressed. With a gesture, no more, this boy makes old things new.

Kashperl leaves his coffee to cool on the counter while he steps out to see where this boy is headed. He seems to know. Down the street he goes to Kashperl's Army Surplus, where he pulls up short to peer in the window. What can he want? He seems to already have all Kashperl sells. Crash helmet, stirrup boots, pants tight in the crotch, tassels on all of the zippered pockets. Gloves, perhaps? New strings for his guitar? To beat the boy to the water fountain, Kashperl comes up so fast his foot stomps the treadle: the jet of water is too strong. Does it explain the paleness of the boy's nose? Water drips from the visor to darken his boots. He blows through wet lips, draws a black hand across a wide, pale mouth. As a boy Kashperl had seen such a mouth on the face of Chatauqua minstrels, as if the unearthly brightness of the smile had bleached the lips. Matter-of-factly Kashperl says, "Saw you looking in the window. Anything special?"

The boy tilts his head to give him a side glance. The amber visor stains the whites of his eyes, but his nose is the color of a metal button. It occurs to Kashperl that he wears the helmet to conceal his unhappy condition. A black boy with a nose that "bleeds," a color that runs.

"What's your name, son?"

"Gainer," he replies, "like in half gainer."

"That's a good name," says Kashperl. "People call you half or whole Gainer?" He does not smile. Is that why Kashperl almost laughs?

"What's so funny?" says the boy, hoisting his pants.

"Mr. Gainer," says Kashperl, "what's your first name?"

"Jubal-eee."

"Your name is Jubalee?"

"E's for Emory. Jubal E. Gainer."

Time was when a man drove a stake into the earth, or ran up a flag, denoting possession. Kashperl can do no more than contain his excitement. "Play anything?" he says.

"I play gee-tar, and High-Five. How much the guns?"

Kashperl grips the lapels of his greatcoat. "All prices, boy. If it shoots, it's not cheap."

"What's not cheap?" Kashperl wheels him slowly, taking a grip on one arm. As they walk toward the Army Surplus there is something in his head, or his helmet, that rattles. "Son—" Kashperl asks him gently, "who you plan to shoot?"

CHAPTER FIVE

The smiling fat man unlocks the door, blocks it open with an army surplus gas can. "Look around, son," he says, and flicks a switch. Ceiling lights blink. On the wall is a collapsible boat, collapsed, a dummy outfitted in a navy flight suit.

"Where the guns?" Jubal asks.

They are in a glass case under the cash register, behind which the fat man stands smiling. He pats his hand on the case. "How about a nice pellet gun. On special."

He disappears behind the case, reappears with the gun. Out of the case, in the open, it looks fierce. It has heft when Jubal lifts it. "It shoots just pellets?"

"Does when it don't clog," says the fat man. He takes the gun from Jubal, disappears with it. "It's a good buy," he says, "but not a good gun."

It's a fact that people will surprise you. Here's one that says what he sells is no good. "What good's a gun that don't shoot?"

"People have wondered, eh, boy?"

Jubal and the fat man appraise each other. He sees that

Jubal is no fool. If he is going to buy a gun, he wants one that shoots. He stoops, once more, behind the counter, then he reappears with a gun that has no barrel. Nor much of anything else.

"To keep the ladies off," he says, and puts it on the counter.

"Who wants to keep the ladies off?" says Jubal.

"Not me," says the fat man.

"Nor me," says Jubal. He steps back from the case to hoist his levis. What would this fat man think if he knew where Jubal got the stains on his knees? The smell of apples?

"What you have in mind to shoot, boy?"

Jubal says, "Hell, you never know who you'll run into. You run into some awful nutty people."

"That you do," says the fat man. "That you do if you got something to lose."

Jubal wonders how he knows what is none of his business. "How much is that one?" he says, and points at it. It is like a six-shooter with the barrel sawed off.

The fat man slips it out from the case. "Holster goes with it. A real piece of armor."

"How much?" says Jubal.

"$38.90. If it shoots, it's not cheap."

Jubal whistles. "I can't swing that."

"Somebody's in luck," says the fat man. "How about a knife?"

Jubal stoops to peer at the tray in the case. The fat man takes it out. They are long-handled switchblades with bone and pearl handles. Jubal once lost one playing touch football. He flicks the blade to show he knows about such knives, the price is on the blade. "$6.98! Kee-rist!"

"Special this week, $4.98. If it cuts it's not cheap."

The knife is lined with brass, has double nickel bolsters, and the word Longhorn stamped on the blade. It's a knife LeRoy Cluett would like to toy with. But it's a knife, not a gun.

"How old are you, son?"

"Me? I'm old enough."

"Sing, dance, or both?" says the fat man.

"Why'd you think I do that?" The fat man shrugs. "Well, I play some, but I don't sing much."

"Who sings, boy? You sure you can't sing? If I knew for sure you couldn't sing, you're hired. If you're old enough."

"I'm nineteen," Jubal lies.

"You're hired," the fat man says. He puts the knife into Jubal's palm. "My compliments."

"Mister, you pullin' my leg?"

The fat man has ducked down behind the counter, the tray of knives on the top. Does he mean to see if Jubal will take one? The handle of the knife that he holds is slippery, his palms are damp. "That rain I hear?" the fat man says. Jubal turns to the door but it is not raining. The mailman is crossing the street with something tinkling on his rubber-tired mailcart. He comes in with several letters that he slaps on the counter. Peering around he says, "You hear the news, Kashperl?"

"On the hour," says the fat man. "I miss it?" His head pops up from behind the counter.

"Holly Stohrmeyer," says the mailman, "some maniac attacked her."

"Did what?"

"Guess he raped her." The fat man makes no comment. The mailman slaps his hand on the counter, says, "What'll they think of next?" That is not so much a question as a statement. He knows the maniac at large will think of something. The fat man says, "They catch him?"

"Ha!" says the mailman. He turns to look through the door. "Know what she says he looks like?"

"A spook," says Kashperl.

"Not bad," says the mailman. "Thinks she saw a space-man. How you like that?"

"She could do worse."

"What I told the Sheriff. Ought to leave him at large as a public service."

"A spaceman," says Kashperl. "Do a lot for the space program if it gets around."

The mailman slaps the counter again, then goes out to his cart. He's a puller, rather than a pusher, and the cart wags like a tail behind him. Wind puffs through the door, blowing a piece of the mail from the counter top to one of the lockers. Kashperl stoops to pick it up. As he opens it he says, "Now why'd a boy like *you* do that?"

Why *did* he? He feels his face will crack if he speaks.

"Now why'd a boy like you do that?" the fat man repeats, as if he was questioning something in the letter.

"You want to know something, mister?"

The fat man doesn't reply. He slips the circular back into the envelope, drops it into the army surplus wastebasket.

"You really want to know something?"

"I know," says the fat man. "This old lady jumped you."

The crazy ways of the world silence Jubal. People are either nutty or they think only evil. If he had just half the sense he was born with he would keep his mouth shut.

"This old lady jumps you, but you manage to fight her off." The fat man sounds as if he were reading it from the letter he has opened.

"She's not so old," says Jubal, "for one thing."

"There's older ones, boy, if that's your taste."

"You want to know something, fat man?" Is Jubal shouting at him? The visor makes an echo chamber of his voice. "I run out of gas. All I wanted was some gas. She was sittin' on the porch with her shirt off, peelin' apples."

"I know," says the fat man, "you're nuts about apples."

"She'd cut herself. She'd cut herself with the knife. She holds it out toward me like a kid, to fix it. How the hell was I to know she was feeble-minded?"

The fat man looks up from the letter he is reading. It leads Jubal to wonder what it is he has said.

"How—? Boy, how *did* you?"

That's a good point, and Jubal can appreciate it. He knew something was wrong by the expression in her eyes, and the way she formed words with her lips but didn't speak them. He knew something was wrong the way she held out her finger for him to kiss, and he sucked it. But that was not what the fat man was waiting to hear. He wanted what Jubal had had without all the trouble. He wanted the cherry, which was actually more than Jubal had got. It's a pleasure for Jubal to string him along, however. In this way he can recover what he'd missed the first time, the bloom of it.

"You want to know something?" he says. It was clear that he did. "She wasn't so old that she didn't enjoy it, fat man. I'd say she got more out of it than I did. You get too friggin' worked up. You got to do all the work. All the woman's got to do is lie there and enjoy it."

"That's an interesting point," says the fat man. "An interesting point."

"You dam right," says Jubal. "She gets most of the fun, and all the poor guy gets is the credit."

"Your credit's good, my boy, see anything else you'd like?"

The fat man turns to wave his small hand at the tables and racks of army surplus. "How about some new pants, a new sweat shirt?"

"What's wrong with the shirt I got?" asks Jubal. He has a special feeling for J. S. Bach. He doesn't like beards. He likes the hair on the head, not the face.

"Nothing at all, son. Nothing at all, but it looks to me like maybe your color is running."

Jubal is not thrown by that. No, he takes that cool as you please. In one sense of the word he has not come far since leaving William Holden in a ditch in Korea: in another sense he has come too far to ever turn back.

"Take your pick," says the fat man. He waves at a table where the sweat shirts come in three bright colors. "Help yourself. Dressing room at the back. While you're at it you might use a little soap, get yourself a new face."

Is it that Jubal doesn't like fat men, or just this one? He means to be friendly. He smiles at Jubal, but the smile is not returned.

"Fat man, I got a new face already. I like the one I got."

"Look, boy—" says the fat man, and comes around the corner with his right arm extended toward Jubal. All he means to do is take Jubal by the arm and turn him around to face a full-length mirror. Let Jubal see for himself just how he looks. The skin around his wide mouth is like pewter given a buff with the wrong kind of polish. The visor gives the color of illness to his eyes and nose. Water that has dripped from his face to his chest has streaked the face of J. S. Bach like black sweat. A twist of apple peel is stuck to his hair. On the face of it he is just the sort of boy to scare the daylights out of a simple-minded woman, suck her cut finger, and then assault her the best he knew how. He is handicapped by a lack of experience, but learning fast. "Look—" says the fat man, but the pudgy hand he extends toward Jubal doesn't quite reach him. Jubal's arm is longer, even without the added length of the knife. He has flicked the blade, then thrust it deep into the fat man's padded shoulder, through the padding into the firm cushion of flesh. But there is no impact. It is the same as goosing a hog. The blade goes to the hilt, as if into foam rubber, but no blood spurts and it comes out clean.

The fat man makes no sound. Nothing shows in his face but astonishment. Jubal waits for him to faint, to cry out, to do something, but he does nothing palpable but breathe. A film of moisture oils his face. There is an army locker on the floor behind him, but it is not clear to Jubal how he knows it. He does not look. He merely sags and folds. Down he goes, as if into quicksand, or as a man stoned by the heat. From this crouch he looks up at Jubal for the first time. He smiles. At what he sees he can't help but smile. Jubal would like to shout what the hell is so funny, but not all of this smile is for Jubal. He shares it with a figure who stands in the door. This boy wears levis scissored at the knees so they will fray out nicely, like the fringe on a buggy. He carries a skateboard. The first drops of rain have splattered his bare feet. He twirls one of the skateboard's wheels. "You got extra wheels?"

"No, son," says the fat man.

The boy neither believes what he hears, or what he sees. He stands there as if warming his motor, his eyes fastened on Jubal. What does he see? Whatever it is it scares him to death. The wheel on the skateboard goes on spinning, but his legs do not move. It is left to Jubal to do what comes naturally: he runs. He goes between the tables piled green with army surplus to the door at the back beneath the open ventilator. When he opens this door rain pings on his helmet, stings cool on his face. He draws his sleeve across the smear on his visor because the light in the alley seems peculiar. The rim of the sky glares like dawn. Overhead it is black. He is never doing more than what comes naturally, but it is amazing how many things seem to. Lights change from red to green as he runs, the wind thrusts at his back. He goes between serried ranks of parked cars toward the seeing-eye doors of the supermarket. One swings inward, as if beckoning: from the other a shopping cart is ejected. It drifts, unchaperoned, down the ramp in his direction. One front wheel wobbles. A bottle rattles inside the cage. Back in the door a woman stands like a bird with clipped wings. One lifts lamely from her side: with the other she waves. She wears a green-tinted plastic raincoat over a dress striped like an awning. Tumbling hair conceals one side of her heart-shaped face. With the cart, which he notes contains one bottle of gin, one carton of cat food, Jubal goes rattling up the ramp toward the woman who has stooped to grope for her hairpins, the heels of both shoes caught in the mat at the door.

███

Has Haffner been assaulted and robbed? Plainly he has been mugged. The skin has been rubbed from the arch of his nose; there are also disturbing prominences elsewhere. But who can say but what they are natural? The lumps behind his ears are strange, but hardly new. That is not true, however, of the wine-dark stains on his chalky teeth.

Hodler sits patiently at the bedside while the intern goes methodically through Haffner's pockets. It is not easy. They are many, including the vest, and the openings are small. Haffner's suits are of British cloth, hand-tailored in Hong Kong. The label inside the jacket is burnished like a coat of arms. Some men carry the future in their pockets, some the past. Hodler cannot abide Haffner's whimsy, his mania for lying, his talent for exaggeration, his perverse sense of nonsense, his love of paradox, his four-in-hand ties, his belief that hoarhound drops will prevent serious chest colds, but if Hodler is a thinking man, and he is, who so well as Haffner fills his idle thoughts? No one. Not even Pauline Bergdahl so often puzzles and stupefies him. And now he will have a glimpse of the inside of Haffner: what makes him tick. The first item proves to be a snuffbox made of horn, stamped *Hecho en México*. And the snuff? It sniffs to Hodler like Sen-Sen.

The intern makes a place on the bedside table, and spreads a towel to keep the objects from rolling.

Three silver linked chains. He has a thing about chains. One clips to his belt and has a pipe tool on it. He does not smoke a pipe. One has keys: house keys, school keys, useless keys, and a rabbit's foot luck charm.

His Volkswagen car keys on a fob with the Jaguar emblem. On the chain is a disc with Haffner's name and address, a request that the finder please drop same in mailbox. This has actually occurred.

A French gas-type lighter, in a leather case. Hodler has always coveted this lighter. The American gas models are not so chic. Haffner, of course, cannot remember how to load it, or replace the flints, or where to buy the refills. It has none now.

Another pipe tool. Italian. Looks like a black lacquered whiskey muddler. Ideal for passing the time. Conversation starter. Haffner uses it for nail cleaner, scalp scratcher, table tapper.

Coins. Haffner carries a silver dollar won by him from a slot machine in Las Vegas. Change he keeps in a coin purse of buffalo hide, most of the coins of foreign vintage. Italian coins he passes off on Pickett parking meters. Greek he keeps for luck.

A watch-like ornament of plastic and metal, on a short chain. Swiss-made, it ticks like a stove timer. It warns you with a buzz about the time on your meter. It gives Hodler the creeps.

Small carbon stone in leather case for sharpening pocket knives. Haffner loses all the knives, but never the stone. Hodler has seen him smooth a snagged fingernail with it. English pigskin. Gift of a student who bought it during stopover at Shannon Airport.

Knife tool in seal-leather case with nail file, nail clipper, scissors, leather punch, magnifier, two-inch ruler, cork puller, can opener, screwdriver, hair tweezers, collar and button hooker, also one broken blade. Haffner uses scissors to clip the tips off filter-tipped cigarettes.

Bill clip made of split Italian coin, no bills. Haffner uses clip jaws to bite his own fingers, snap like a dog at passing (pretty) students.

Billfold of alligator plastic, gift of insurance salesman, accordion file of plastic pockets contain snapshots of friends, newspaper clippings, theater stubs, and scented tissue for removing excess oil from facial pores. Haffner has it.

Also a small dented capsule of yellow plastic which the intern carefully opens, sniffs. Contains flints. Flints for a lighter he has lost, given free with a pack of cigarettes.

His money is in the watch pocket of his pants. A tight-folded wad of six one-dollar bills.

"Hey!" says the intern. "No watch. He steal your watch?"

There is a pause. Haffner shrugs. "Maybe I forget it."

If nothing much seems to be wrong with him, what is *right?* The blood-red cherry juice rinsed from his hair, his face, he looks the same. But how explain what that is? He wears a flannel nightshirt. The stain of the cherries gives the smear of life to his lips. It is no concern of his that Hodler eyes him like a species defying classification. The name is Haffner. All Haffners are one of a kind. Hodler is free to leave the room and go about his business, which is proving, hourly, to be considerable, or to sit on a folding chair and study Haffner. So he sits on the chair. In the last few minutes the wind has veered. Now it puffs from the north. The elms he sees through the blinds wave like plumes or plants growing underwater. Hodler finds it soothing. The rasp of the gasoline saw has stopped. In the clearing where the elm had stood citizens have gathered as if at a burial. Hodler cannot think what day it is. He is ashamed to ask.

The mugged one, Haffner, has had his shots, and they might well explain the flush of health in his cheeks. His head is browless: his nose terminates the curvature of his spine. Hodler has often wondered how he would look without his feathers. A myna bird with rickets, the eyelids painted. Haffner's skull, like a caveman's stone ax, is wedged at an angle between his hunched shoulders. Every movement of his head flattens the lobes of his ears. When he speaks Hodler glimpses the lining of the spout-like lower lip, like an inflamed eyelid. Ugly as sin. In many ways as likable.

The intern says, "Anything missing, Mr. Haffner?"

Haffner taps a finger on his blue-veined temple. The young man is not surprised. He holds that opinion privately. He is a clean-cut boy with small attractive features, the bright, ready smile of a man proud of his dentures. Through the furze of his flat-top his scalp gleams like a glass egg. Not at all Hodler's type, but nevertheless he behaves. He does not mug old men or set up traps for small children. He does not drop from space to have his way with old ladies, or pervert college boys. Is it the law? Is it something he possesses or something he lacks? The intern says, "Well, just so you didn't lose more than the time, eh?" He guffaws.

Haffner is not a man without his standards. Solemnly he plucks at the lint on his nightshirt, as if for fleas. Hodler says, "First he jumps Miss Holly, then you. Besides a spaceman, just what's he look like?"

Haffner beams like a dog whose back is being scratched.

"Funny, eh?" Hodler goes on. "Not everybody is going to find him so funny. He's still at large. He's still on the loose——"

"On the loose?"

"As of now," says Hodler. He glances at his watch to check that. Eleven minutes till noon. Five minutes later than Hodler's usual gallop for lunch.

"Poy on the loose!" Haffner repeats, and the idea delights him. He moves his fingers through the air like a swimming minnow. He darts his hand to the left, toward Hodler, then he dips under a rock. Hodler ponders what it would be like to have him sick in the house. "Poy on the loose!" he repeats.

"Very funny," says Hodler. "You think the next victim will find it so funny?"

"Coot be." He gives Hodler the glance of a tipsy satyr.

"You're not going to tell me what he looks like?"

"Loogs like?" Haffner pretends to ponder. What he sees on his mind's eye tilts his head to wagging. Can't he bear to describe it? It pains him to laugh, but he is laughing. He draws his knees to his chest and hugs them. The sound he makes is that of squeezing air from an inner tube. It is not at all difficult for Hodler to grasp why this peculiar-looking spaceman crowned him with a sack of cherries. Why just cherries? Why not something more impressive? Hodler is a sober man, but for this boy on the loose, free to indulge in his whims, he feels a twinge of envy. There is something to be said for impulsive behavior, although Hodler is perhaps not the man to say it. Visiting spacemen are free to act in a way he is not. The soreness of his ribs is a torment to Haffner, but he continues to laugh. Hodler rises and says, "I'll see you later!" It is almost a shout. The door to the room, however, is blocked by a short, wide man who holds a mug of black coffee. He too looks like a spaceman on the loose. A stethoscope plugs his ears. He pulls the tubes from his ears, says, "You people hear that?"

At the far end of the hall Hodler can hear the voice of the Pickett newscaster, but not what he says. "Predictable," says the man, "typical sort of twist. He gets the taste of blood then he gets sexy." He takes a swig of the coffee then repeats, "Typical sort of twist."

Hodler realizes this is Dr. McCain, on a one-semester loan from a clinic in Cleveland. He moves from the door to let Hodler pass, then follows him down the hall to the water cooler. He has another swig of the coffee while Hodler drinks. "Perversion—" he says, getting Hodler's attention, "derives from tendency to rough the little girl up a little. Love-bite, dog-bite. Not too much difference. Soon it's the dog-bite he wants."

Hodler stands sipping the tepid water, toying with the paper cup. He can't bear to drink so little, then throw the cup away. Now he rests it on top of the cooler in the hope that some kid will come along and use it, never having heard of germs.

"Bit of the mad dog in us all, eh, Hodler?"

McCain has what Hodler thinks of as good strong choppers. He would make a good dog. The mad dog in Hodler is not on the surface, but McCain knows it is there, and he finds it reassuring, almost comforting. He gives Hodler a casual slap on the seat, heads back down the hall. The noon whistle blows on the roof of the firehouse and Hodler stands, feeling a trembling in his thighs, as he listens to the ominous weather forecast: the barometer is falling. More rain is expected with rising winds. More trouble is expected from the spaceman, still on the loose.

CHAPTER SIX

Let me, Ma'am——" he says, and drops to his knees. Not only hairpins: cigarettes have spilled from the open pack in her raincoat pocket. The golf-tee heels of both shoes are stuck in the mat. "Let me," he says, and tries to take a grip on the shoe without touching the ankle. She wears no stockings: a soiled Band-Aid protects a blister between her toes. Water flicked by the heels of the shoes spreckel her calves. The heels have triangular metal caps that push through a hole but resist pulling out. Looking up he says, "Ma'am, maybe you better take it off."

In the shelter of the rain hood her face is heart-shaped, clouded with smoke. In the shadow of the helmet his is like that of a stoker at an open porthole.

"Fresh!" she says.

With his white-knuckled black hands he fumbles at the shoe strap, pulls it tighter.

"Ouch!" she cries. Tumbling hair conceals her face as she stoops, more hairpins fall. He gropes for the pins and she loosens the shoe strap to slip out her foot, curl up the wet toes. One of her hands rests on his shoulder. He gives the shoe a twisting wrench; the heel pops off. A woman

with a cart who stands waiting to pass hoarsely laughs.
Jubal holds in his left hand the heelless shoe while she shifts
her weight to the shoeless foot. The mat is prickly. The
weight is shifted back. Before Jubal can move or speak she
gives the foot a jerk, snapping the strap. Both her bare
feet are now on the mat. He has never before been so
close to such flat ones. The seeing-eye door thumps him in
the rear as she steps from the mat, goes off with the cart.
When he straightens up, both shoes in his hands, she is
walking the cart through the blowing drizzle, her feet
slapping the asphalt. With her hair down like that she is
like a big kid. The wobbly wheel of the cart will not go
straight, pulling it out of line. Beside her he says, "You
like me to take it?" but she likes it the way it is. She likes
slapping her feet in the puddles, pushing a cart. He carries
the shoes like a wino carries bottles, tucked up his sleeves.
Why doesn't he put them into the cart? He likes it the
way it is. The smooth curve of the arches are cool on the
palms of his hands.

They stand in the drizzle waiting for the light to
change.

She lifts her eyes to the light, flicking from red to
green, then looks down the street to the white Porsche
parked at a meter where the time has expired. Chained to
the post of the meter is the guitar and the wet army duffle.

"We're double-parked!" she says.

What can he say to that? If anything, he will think of it
later. At the moment he is thinking she would be even
taller if she had on her shoes. A man coming toward them
in a yellow slicker suddenly stops, as if startled. One hand

swings up to the brim of his hat. He looks like a cop. But it is only Alan Hatfield, whose eyes are better than his wife's. His jaw hangs slack as he looks from Jubal to her gleaming feet. Her arms, without warning, suddenly lift from her sides as if she would fly, and her hands flutter. Only a moment, but long enough for the cart, tilted on the curb, to spill the cat food and the gin into the street. Alan Hatfield comes running, but the red light stops him. Jubal Gainer, the green light with him, his helmet bobbing to the rhythm of his canter, goes off pawing the air like a circus horse, well-shoed on all fours.

As Hodler crosses the square grackles dive at his head and the wind has veered around to blow from the east. He stoops twice to pick up empty beer cans, once for a Diet Cola bottle full of cigarette butts, the tips smeared with lipstick. He is pained and pleased at once. The bottle will supply him with an editorial. The thoughtful coed who leaves her butts in the bottle, the swain who leaves the bottle and the cans on the greensward. Hodler has a column, "The Skin of Our Teeth," which he fills with such thought-provoking items. A college smart aleck has described him as having a very litteral mind.

On Clay Street Hodler walks toward the corner litter basket, a civic-minded improvement brought about by his efforts. At the noon hour all the parking spaces are filled but the one in front of the *Courier* office. The stall is vacant, but the meter is occupied. A dark green army duffle, and what might be a guitar, are fastened to the meter post with a length of cable, the ends padlocked. This is just the sort of story Hodler prizes, but it is no story at all without a picture of it. His camera, of course, he has left in his car. And his car? It is parked off the highway, the windows cranked down, the keys in the ignition. But the motor off. He does make it a habit of turning the motor off.

He drops the cans and the bottle in the litter basket, then waits at the curb reserved for McPhail's taxi service. People Hodler knows pass him by in both directions, but he does not wave. The simplest situations are often the hardest to explain. Hodler in town, his car a mile out of town, word of Miss Holly's rape now all over town—Hodler could easily explain, but it would take time, and one way or another it would lead to complications. McPhail, a chronic liar and windbag, would be bad enough. Hodler also had the problem of remaining impartial, which he can manage well enough while waiting. Impartially he watches the light change from red to green, and hears the hoot of the horns when there is no traffic movement. The motor has stalled in Sanford Avery's battered pickup. He leans out of the cab to flag his arm: he puts his head out to ask the car behind to push him. It does. Hodler watches as they cross the intersection, in tandem. The power-mower is still roped to the back of the cab, but the driver has shaved. Perhaps he looks forward to being photographed, while interviewed. They go down the street to the first parking stall, which proves to be the green zone in front of the post office.

Hodler cannot abide Avery, but it means a free ride, the minimum of explanation, the maximum of information. He watches Avery, spread-legged, trot across the street and go through the open door to the firehouse. The Sheriff is there. His patrol car is parked at the curb out in front. Hodler strolls down the street to take a seat in the pickup, which is a boon to Avery since he has left the motor running. The cab smells of the chickens Avery dresses on the farm, puts in pails of water, then delivers in town. The cracked windshield has been repaired with a bolt and a round piece of plywood. The blade of the wiper has not wagged for several months. Hodler is a great one to admire the old cars a man could keep going with a pair of pliers and some hairpins, but to ride or sit in one is always something of a shock. How they vibrate! How do they smoke without burning? He leans out of the cab to breathe. The scene directly before him, screened by the splintered and vibrating window, Hodler does not observe until a boy with a skateboard, who has been yelling, goes off up the alley with a rasping snort. Eight or ten people, Pickett citizens and students, stand in a clutter at the door to Kashperl's Army Surplus. Two steps go up to the door, which stands open, and Hodler sees the huge Kashperl, passive as a Buddha, seated on one of his surplus army lockers, propped up by his own knees. One man has stepped forward to speak to him, repeating his name. If Hodler sees at all clearly, which is unlikely, Kashperl smiles in the manner of Miss Holly. Is he ill or drunk? His head lolls loosely to one side. The man who

102

speaks to him turns and shouts, "An ambulance! Get an ambulance!"

Only Hodler moves. The crowd at the front stands at attention while one of their number snaps several pictures. Flashbulbs flash. He holds the apparatus over their heads. It gives Hodler time to climb out of the pickup and approach the scene in a professional manner. "Excuse me," he says, but too late. He is part of the picture the photographer snaps. "Excuse me," he repeats, and they make way for him: the man blocking the door stands aside to admit him. The huge Kashperl is squatted on the sagging tin lid of his smallest locker. There is no sign of struggle. His clothes are neat. His tie hangs straight. His face is the usual sallow, off-white, but the long upper lip is beaded with moisture, the premature shadow on the jowls more ashen than blue. One pudgy hand rests on his knee, the other hangs between his legs, gripping a toy-like pistol. Has he shot himself? No holes or blood are visible. It seems to Hodler that he wears the smile of the peace, or the folly, that passeth understanding: in such extremities of wisdom there was little to choose. To Miss Holly he bears more than a passing likeness. Hodler makes a blind stab at it. "You missed him?"

Kashperl gives him a fond but sad smile. "Yup," he says, Western style, "I missed him," and looks at the weapon that weighs his hand. A lady's? It has a smooth pearl handle. Perhaps the criminal mistook it for a lighter.

"This kid," blurts Hodler, "what's he look like?"

One might have thought Hodler was his accomplice.

Kashperl's broad, morning powdered face wears an amused, benign, resigned expression. He smiles. He seems to find Hodler's question puzzling. "Goddam it!" Hodler cries, "what does this maniac look like?" He has an impulse to give Kashperl a shake, but he controls it. The man's head lolls, as if tipsy, then his entire torso tips over toward Hodler, rests on his thighs. Hodler props him up firmly. "You sick?" Kashperl is at peace with his discomfort. Hodler looks up for help, one hand beckoning, to see Sheriff Cantrill filling the door. He wears his gloves. He stands spread-legged with both hands poised on wide hips. The Sheriff has not been trained in tactics, and it is clear that he looks on Hodler with suspicion. Hodler says, "He's passed out!"

"No kidding," says the Sheriff.

The man who stepped outside to let Hodler in, peers in and says, "He's been stabbed, Mr. Hodler."

Both this man and the Sheriff step to one side to let two white-clad interns in with a stretcher. Hodler sees the ambulance at the curb and the pale glow of the revolving beacon. He steps aside while one of the interns stands behind Kashperl, and supports him, while the other spreads the flap of his coat and probes the narrow clean slit in the jacket fabric, a hand's breadth from the lapel. The slit is as clean as that for a button. Kashperl has been stabbed, but no blood shows. The Sheriff stoops to take the pistol from Kashperl's limp hand and flips it open to look at the empty cartridge. "Shoots peanuts?" he scoffs. Hodler risks no reply. He keeps his blinking eyes on the street, where the crowd stands, and the door through which they carry Kashperl, the two interns at the front of the stretcher, the Sheriff at the foot. A husky college boy, in a red Pickett sweat shirt, gives the Sheriff a hand. The bird-billed head of Avery appears in the doorway and stares, the jaw slack, at Hodler.

"For chrissakes!" he bellows. "Just told the Sheriff you were next! Saw your goddam car!"

Does Hodler smile? The expression he wears crimps the skin around his eyes, cracks his chapped lips. "There's still time," he says, "there's still plenty of time. If nobody is going to say what the hell he looks like."

"Know what I heard?" croaks Avery.

The ambulance siren wails before he can say. It goes off to the south to avoid the intersection, and Hodler follows its course on the faces of the spectators. The Sheriff is one of them: he turns and says, "Anybody here see what happened?" He takes from his pocket a small spiral-bound notebook.

"Customer stabbed him," says a voice.

"You see him? What'd he look like?"

"I didn't see him. Kid with a skateboard told me."

"I saw that boy with the skateboard," says Hodler.

"Some getaway!" says another. "Kid on a goddam skateboard."

Didn't anybody want to pin this public enemy down? Hodler listened to the voices kidding the Sheriff, giving him flat he-went-that-a-way answers. Did they all dream of being a man on the loose? Envied by inhibited red-

105

blooded men, pursued by comical galoots like the Sheriff. He went that-a-way. With the thoughts, fantasies, and envious good wishes of them all.

Hodler closed the doors, then stood under Kashperl's awning waiting for a letup in the downpour. The street had emptied. The windshields of the cars reflected a low, turbulent sky. Would this curtail or expand the goings-on of the man at large? He probably knew as little about that as Hodler, maybe less. Pauline Bergdahl had the word for it, as usual. "Mr. Hodler," she would say, "it's how the cookie crumbles." When it rained it would crumble one way, another when dry. Down where the rain bounced like hail on the sidewalk it blackened the canvas of the army duffle, and pelted the green plastic case of the guitar. The time on the meter was now up. Hodler can see the word EXPIRED when the lightning flickers, and that the car now parked there is Alan Hatfield's Porsche, the wagging wiper leaving an arching rainbow smear on the windshield. In the adjoining stall Mrs. Pauline Bergdahl backs from the cab of the Bergdahl pickup, her feet in a pair of her son's soiled, unlaced tennis shoes.

▄▄▄

"Now why'd he want to go and rape anybody?"

Pauline Bergdahl puts the question to herself and Hodler, who sits behind his desk. She doesn't mean it to be idle. Rape is one of those things she finds puzzling. In the hills south of Pickett there are girls to be had without all of that mess and trouble, as well as boys who prefer that a girl should collaborate. Hodler gives her time to reflect on the matter while he rubs at the specks on his glasses. He squints with one eye like a watch repairman. He puts the lens in his wide mouth and softly exhales. The smoke that hangs between them—something to do with the weather, the sense of pressure that gives Hodler a head-ache—does not rise and billow around the ceiling fan but sags in spots as if heavy. Heavy it is with the smell of Hodler's pipe. The exact nature of this scent had escaped Hodler until classified by Pauline Bergdahl. Night after night he sat in her diner, smoking his pipe. The fan in the kitchen sucked this smoke through the food slot that framed the head and arms of Mrs. Bergdahl, her chin propped on the dish towel that was always twisted around her left hand. Every day she smelled it. One day she solved it.

"That mixture smells like a wet hound dog, Mr. Hod-ler."

This was not in distaste, since she owned two of them, but merely another aspect of her natural talent: to pin down an illusive, vagrant impression gave Pauline Berg-dahl a keen sense of pleasure. It also made her up to forty dollars in a busy month. Through the food slot in the diner, and the windows that faced the highway, she saw the strange in the familiar and the familiar in the strange. The five dollars Hodler paid her for what he printed in no way measured the importance of her contribution.

"Pauline," he'd often say, "you like to run a news-paper?"

"Then I'd be like you an' with no time to read it."

Hodler not only likes this woman, he is drawn to her. Her hair is coarse and black as a mule's tail, her skin is like hide, the color of ripe tobacco, her lips are chapped, her shanks are lean, her breasts lob in a sling she makes of flour sacks, but she is a woman and Hodler is aware that he is a man when she sits and stares at him. He is grateful for the cloud of smoke, for the shelter of his desk. He cannot see her legs but he knows that one is twisted like a vine around the other, both dirty feet slipped out of her younger son's tennis shoes. She is accident-prone. Her arms are scarred with burns and she often smells like a freshly singed chicken. Without the diner shelf to lean on she cups one elbow in the palm of one hand, her chin is cupped in the other: the fingers pluck at her chapped lips, or drum on her false teeth. She has "cases" of nerves, chews her nails to the quick, is often known to be mean as a mink in a pen, but when Hodler thinks of people in their natural state—when he thinks of it as being a good one—he thinks of Pauline Bergdahl. Her name is Pauline, but from an early age her husband has called her Pearly, after *The Perils of Pauline*. She was born in the woods that stretch behind the diner, had a good education up through spelling and fractions, fries all of her eggs hard on both sides and serves them with ketchup poured on the French fries. Her coffee comes with the spoon in it, a film of grease on the top.

"Now why'd he want to go and knife anybody—if he wasn't provoked?"

"Do you knife a person if he crosses you, Pauline?"

"I wouldn't want to cross Melvin, if he's moody."

Pauline's oldest boy, Melvin, aged nineteen, has been

married two years and has three daughters. He is of interest to Hodler as the only teenager he personally knows with a set of false teeth. He hunts coons, does road work, and fishes. Day in and day out, summer and winter, he wears a hunting cap with red flannel earmuffs on the outside. When Hodler tried to persuade him to stay in high school he replied that he had to help his daddy with the farmin'. Thirty acres of this farm are in scrub and woods, seven in soybeans. Bergdahl plows this land with two old horses that wear straw hats to keep the sun off, nets to keep the flies off, and rest for ten minutes at the end of each furrow where they stand in the shade and eat mulberries. The remainder of Bergdahl's farming is to shell a little popcorn and put out a few traps.

"You think you understand these kids, Pauline?"

"They ain't a mean bunch at heart, Mr. Hodler."

"Not unless you cross 'em, eh, Pauline? Is it crossin' 'em that makes 'em ornery?"

Humor is not one of Pauline's strong points. She does not return Hodler's smile as she considers the import of what he has said. They watch the campus trees blow. Rain splatters the windows as if from a hose. Hodler glances up to see clouds blowing like wash on a line. Through the gaps ripped by the wind another sky is visible, the surface rippled but tranquil.

Hodler says, "He wants a new bike, so he takes it. He wants a woman, so he rapes her. He wants a ride so he mugs the driver. He wants a gun so he knifes Mr. Kashperl—" The mention of Kashperl is a mistake. A large segment of her simple uncluttered nature is a simple-minded uncluttered dislike of all Jews. They cause wars.

They run the country. An actress had to sleep with them if she wanted to be famous. Pauline got her information from a Christian scholar who broadcast it after midnight from Nacogdoches, Texas. She sent him two dollars a month. "He don't mean to be mean," says Hodler, "he just takes what he wants."

Pauline Bergdahl's gaze is out the window where her husband and one son sit in the cab of the pickup. Several fishing poles block the door on the driver's side. Hodler can barely see their weathered faces through the rain-streaked dirt on the windshield. Chicken and grackle droppings whiten the hood. The tail of a coon shot by one of the boys is fastened to the radiator, and lifts in the wind gusts.

"They don't mean no meanness, Mr. Hodler, and they don't mean no goodness either. They just couldn't care less."

What disturbs Hodler the most? What she has said, or that she knows it? "If that's true——" he begins, but he checks to watch a banner, stretched over the sidewalk, pull loose from its mooring. In the wind it blows out like a flag, and he can read the rippling message as if on water.

THE BEATLES
HELP!

Hodler waits for Mrs. Bergdahl to make some comment, but the wind drops and the banner collapses. "If that's true, Pauline," he repeats, "where does that leave us?"

"Leave them, you mean? They don't know more'n what they think, Mr. Hodler."

One of Hodler's problems with Mrs. Bergdahl is the extent to which she knows what she is saying. Does Hodler? That he knows *less* than what he thinks is why his thinking is such a torment. The metal sign that hangs above his door rocks in the wind like a tolling bell. Mrs. Bergdahl sits with her fingers to her lips as if feeling a scar. Calmly she says, "It's twister weather."

"That's a forecast?" Hodler smiles. People are always calling to forecast the weather, especially if it's bad.

"It was a twister I first reported," says Pauline.

Hodler has forgotten, but it seems reasonably likely.

"It's the season——" he begins, but she interrupts him.

"Truth to tell, I think it wasn't, Mr. Hodler. It wasn't a forecast, it was a news report. The twister went right by on Route 'leven. A horse in it, over on his side like he was swimmin' underwater. A lovely sight."

"Lovely?" Hodler echoes, just checking.

"The will of God," she says, "you have to see it." She pauses to give him time to. "To make loaves out of fishes, Mr. Hodler. To make nails out of straw——"

A man who knows less than he thinks, but thinks, Hodler says, "To make a shambles of a town is not lovely, Mrs. Bergdahl."

"The shambles ain't but it's the will to do it. Who you think gives the twist to the wind, Mr. Hodler, the movie folks?"

The twist to the argument silences Hodler. He sits, his

pipe dead, watching the wind blow. The leaves on the elm felled that morning show their backsides and look frosted. He doesn't know if the sound he hears is thunder or a passing jet. He doesn't know, that is, if it is the will of God or man. The horn of the pickup at the curb toots twice, and Mrs. Bergdahl rises, her rain slicker cracking. Hodler walks ahead of her to open the door. The air does not puff in, as usual, but sucks the smoke out of Hodler's office. A wreath of it trails along with Mrs. Bergdahl to where her son Clarence holds the pickup door open. He gives his mother a push on the bottom to help her climb in. Hodler dimly sees her hand waving as they drive off.

Lightly splattered with rain, the duffle bag and the guitar are still chained to the adjoining parking meter. He notes that the car parked in the space is still the Hatfields' Porsche, sometimes described by scoffers as a skateboard. It is as low, and when given the gun makes about as much noise. Rain and wet leaves smear the windshield, the hood steams as if hot. It's not unusual for Hodler, as a neighborly gesture, to drop coins in the meters for citizens who are known to be forgetful. Alan Hatfield is one. Hodler too would be forgetful if he had a young woman like Charlotte Hatfield to contend with. In her nearsighted way she had mistaken Hodler for her husband on several occasions. Alan Hatfield is the overly casual California type who sometimes lectured in his combat boots, and Hodler has seldom seen him wearing anything but his faded pea jacket, his hands weighting the pockets. Not Hodler's type. That was hardly sufficient reason, of course, to stand by and let him get a parking ticket.

Hodler dips a hand into his pocket, feeling for coins. As he stands sorting out the pennies someone seated in the car gives a toot on the horn. Is that for Hodler? He thinks so. Just what he would expect from Charlotte Hatfield. There she sits in the car, with the meter expired, content to wait until she sees somebody with pennies. Of course it would be Hodler. Hodler to the rescue in the rain. He flags his hand to indicate he has the message, then canters through the rain to the meter. Through the smear on the windshield he sees the glow of her cigarette. He inserts three pennies, soaking up the downpour, then he wheels and runs for his office. Before he reaches it she gives another long toot on the horn. Was that in thanks? It is followed by another. Hodler pauses in the door to marvel at her. She has opened the flap of the side curtain to put out her arm, frantically wave it. At who? It is not for Hodler. It waves and beckons in the opposite direction. Hodler leans out to peer down the street for Alan, but the rain-swept sidewalk is empty. Not a soul. Nothing but the squares of light in front of the shops. Near the corner, however, a gangling, helmeted galoot stands in the shelter of the movie marquee. It saddens Hodler to think he is the first in line for *Help!* Surely there is nothing in this world he needed more. Against the peculiar glow of the sky he resembles something new in street lamps, the wet globe of the helmet gleaming with an eerie, reflected light. His shoulders are darkly wet. There is no room in his tight-assed pants for his dangling hands. One of them—as Hodler stares—half-heartedly raises as if waving to some-one. Could it be Hodler? He peers around. He could only be waving to the silly Charlotte, her hair wet and blowing, her white arm sticking out of her raincoat sleeve. What could she want with the boy under the awning? He too seems to wonder. He glances down the street at his back, then turns back to point a doubting finger at himself. Yes, it is him that she wants. What for? Hodler watches her arm lower to point toward the meter, where the duffle and the guitar are still chained, then twist to wag at the luggage rack on the back of the car. The idle tumblers of Hodler's mind are slow to unlock this message: they get it, but they prefer to let the door open by itself. The duffle and the guitar belong to this boy, and Charlotte Hatfield is offering him a ride. Alan, wearing one of Kashperl's surplus army raincapes, comes from the alley behind the market with a carton of groceries. He puts it in the car, on the shelf behind the seat, then he stands in the rain listening to Charlotte, turning, as she talks, to look in the direction of the movie marquee. So does Hodler, leaning into the rain to see that the awning now shelters no one. The boy in the white helmet runs for the corner, if that is the word to describe his crippled canter, where, in spite of the gusty downpour, he pulls up short when the light changes to red. There he waits, a remarkable example of a responsible, law-abiding citizen, until the green flashes on giving him the all-clear up ahead. Behind a blowing squall of rain that dims the traffic light, slaps like hail on the cars, stings the face of Hodler, and blackens the green duffle chained to the post of the meter, he disappears. By the time Hodler looks back to the parking meter the Hatfield car is gone.

CHAPTER SEVEN

He runs until he's winded. The stirrup heels of his boots sink into the muck, come out with a slurp. He carries his arms like a winded chicken and in a lull in the wind he smells his own sweat. But the rain washing his face tastes of soot rather than salt. He has learned from experience that the problems of survival lie beyond William Holden, the army and the navy. War is crazy, surely, but it seems less crazy than peace. He does not hear the car come up and go by, but he sees, up ahead of him, the glow of the stoplight. It looks warm in the drizzle. He finds the glow of it comforting. The car has pulled to a stop off the road, and he wades in the ditch weeds to go around it. When the door swings open he sees the flat feet in a pair of men's socks.

"Hi!" she says.

"Is that him?" asks the driver. The dashboard lights up his face as he dips his head to look at Jubal. "Like a lift?"

"No sir," says Jubal.

The light behind her, all he sees of her face are the loops of the earrings tapping her cheeks. She edges over in the seat to make room for him, gives it a pat. Her dark mouth is like a bull's-eye in her white face.

"Thanks anyhow," he says, backs away, then walks on ahead. The car just sits there: in the glare of the lights he can see how hard it is raining. His shadow opens before him like a hole in the rain-pocked road. He hears the driver say, "You *might* ask him for your shoes."

The woman laughs. She doesn't speak, she just laughs. Jubal is far up the road, under the drip of trees, before the car starts up and goes slowly past him. He sees the heart-shaped face at the window, the small wagging hand. The cloud of the exhaust veils off the car's stoplight but at the next intersection it turns off the highway: he can follow the bounce and veiled flicker of the lights through the screen of trees. It goes back to where the headlights are reflected in the dark wall of patio windows. He sees the man's shadow loom on the door of the garage, the rain falling in the headlamps, blowing like snow. Lights fill up the garage, then come on in the house. They light up the flagstone patio like the wings of a stage. He stands in the sheltering drip of the trees waiting for the play, watching the movement of the actors: the flames of the fire cast shadows like dancers on the walls. What next? At the thought of it, he laughs. All this time he has been on the run from something: what he feels now is the pull of something. Rain drips from his visor to streak his face. On a puff of the wind he hears the bleat of a horn, he sees the twirling, swirling figure of the dancer whose shoes coolly arch against the moist palms of his hands.

A curious thing about Hodler, a quiet peace-loving man, is the way he loves storms that are often destructive. Windstorms, hailstorms, thunder and lightning, small twists in the wind. He likes bad weather more than he does the good. He likes a big snow. He loves a big flashing line storm. He will go without sleep to watch the streaks of forked lightning. It would be wrong to say he likes a big, roaring twister, since he knows that all twisters are potentially killers. Hodler has strong principles against all killers. They give him no choice. That proves to be a fortunate thing because if left with a choice he would have his problems. He likes the sporting of nature. He likes the idea of a world ruled by nature's Gods. He is saddened by the thought of the cloud-seeders who will one day take the twist out of the twisters, the fear out of the storm. It is a paradox in Hodler's gentle nature and a fortunate thing that his principles give him no choice.

"You kidding?" Kashperl says. He twists on his lips one of the three cigars that Hodler has brought him.

"Just asking," Hodler says, "who gives the twist to the wind?"

"I give up," says Kashperl. It seems a curious remark from such a monumental figure. Hodler cannot resist the impression that Kashperl, martyred, is pulling rank on him.

"I understand," Hodler says, "they can now track them on radar."

"Track what?"

"Twisters."

"Think that's where he'll turn up next?"

Hodler wonders if Kashperl has misunderstood him. "He who?"

"*Him.* If he's still on the loose maybe that's where we'll see him, on the goddam screen!"

A flash of lightning is followed by thunder, the sound pounding the earth like a sonic boom. Hodler is thinking how much twisters are like some people. They liked open spaces. They didn't like cities and crowding. They didn't like fenced-in situations. They needed space to twist in, hop, skip and jump in, room to pull up, to tear down, to raise hell in. In the cities debris would soon clog up the nozzle the way hair and lint clogged up a vacuum cleaner.

"I got a theory," says Kashperl, "just come to me. One man's twister is another man's vacuum. Kashperl's Law. How you like it?" Hodler is in no mood for such horseplay. "Know what nature abhors, Hodler?—a vacuum. Know what a man on the loose heads for? A vacuum. Know what we all fear and admire so much? A vacuum. Now if you just happen to know who has a big one, that's where he'll turn up."

"Who'll turn up, Kashperl?" Hodler turns from the window to look at Sheriff Cantrill, framed in the doorway. Rain drips from the plastic snood that covers his hat. Miss Boyle, the nurse, nudges him out of the door to flick the switch on the wall: the overhead lights flicker. The Sheriff takes a spiral notebook from his jacket pocket, a ball-point pen with the cap missing. He puts the ball-point to his lips, says again, "Who's that'll turn up next?"

"Ma'am——" Hodler says to Miss Boyle, "do you mind if I smoke?"

"Soon as I leave you can do as you please," she replies. She leaves, closing the door with a click.

"It's what they do to put you back on your feet," says Kashperl. No clinic nightshirt will cover his expanse, so he wears his customary T-shirt. There is a bandage no larger than a stamp covering his wound. If he is in pain or discomfort there is no sign of it. Perhaps it is the shots that have done something for him: more than they should.

"You got a theory," says the Sheriff, "right? Okay, shoot." He flips the top page of the spiral notebook, scratches the ball-point to get it started. "You tell me he looks like a spaceman, chum, and I'll personally put you into orbit." He doesn't smile. It is clear that the events of the day are beginning to weigh on Sheriff Cantrill. Particularly the events that have not yet occurred. He has begun a scratchy doodle on the top of the page. "Okay," he says, "shoot."

"I asked for it," says Kashperl, "and I got it." He spreads his small tapered hands before the Sheriff, palms up.

"Continue," says the Sheriff.

"To make a long story short," continues Kashperl, "first we look at some shooting irons, but they run a little high. So we look at some knives, special this week only. Taylor came in with the mail, said, 'You hear the news?

119

Some maniac has raped Holly Stohrmeyer.' He left and I said, 'Now why'd a boy like you do that?' How was I to know he'd done it?"

The Sheriff continues to doodle at the top of the page. At a point vague as the Mason-Dixon line, but as certain, he had stopped believing all that he heard. From the pack in his shirt he flicks a crushed cigarette, goes through his jacket searching for matches. He accepts the pack Hodler offers, smokes with veiled eyes.

"One little thing," he says, "this boy knife you, or did he hold the knife and you run into it?"

Kashperl welcomes the complication. He puts a finger to the flesh of his nose, thinking.

"That's a nice twist," he says, "the twists are for Hodler."

"Did I miss something?" says the Sheriff.

It pains Kashperl to shrug, but he shrugs. "Hodler's Twist, a supplement to Kashperl's Law. You plan to take the twist out of the boy, or out of the wind?"

"I plan to sit here till I get the story," says the Sheriff. "You going to tell me what he looks like?"

"How about a highschool dropout?" says Kashperl. "Two-toned model, one on the lean side. Fond of old ladies, stirrup-heel boots, and Johann Sebastian Bach."

"Would you say he played the gee-tar?" put in Hodler.

"High-Five, too," replies Kashperl. "A versatile talent. Walks like a cowpoke leading a tired horse."

The Sheriff retracts the ball-point of the pen, carefully folds the spiral notebook. He unzips a pocket to slip it away, zips it shut. "You know who needs the protection?" He looks from Kashperl to Hodler. "Me an' that kid. It's me an' that kid who need the protection."

"You know, Sheriff," says Kashperl, "that's what he said! That's why he wanted that gun."

The Sheriff can believe it. He is fully prepared to believe the worst. The lights in the ceiling flicker, the walls in the room seem to be vibrating. Thunder and lightning. Hodler thinks of the names of reindeer. The Venetian blinds cast bars of light on Kashperl so that he looks like a happy convict: a Buddha that grins. The nurse puts in her head and says, "You still here?"

"No," says the Sheriff.

Kashperl says, "Any news?" He licks his lips.

"Don't you just wish there was!" Miss Boyle gives the light switch a flick to stop the flickering. Now they were off. Now they were off and would not come on. "It serves you right," she says, and waits at the door for the visitors to leave.

Hodler pauses in the lobby to slip on his raincoat, snap the noisy galoshes-type buckles. It reminds him that he bought this coat from Kashperl, surplus of some sort. The Sheriff has a swig of water from the cooler, then crushes the cup that Hodler would have spared, drops it into the pail. He precedes Hodler through the clinic doors, and strides toward the car he has left at the curbing, switches his radio on. The voice of the announcer informs them both that they are now having twister weather. One has been spotted east of Ridley, sixty miles to the south. He reminds them all that the safest place is in the basement of the house, or the southwest corner. That gives Hodler no choice. He has rented his house, and the room in which he lives faces the northeast.

The house in which Hodler lives has a fine, dry basement, but the landlady has turned it into a game room. Hodler would rather face the twister than the Kluger girls and their friends. It so happens that his room is on that side of the house certain to vanish in thin air if the twister strikes it, so it is better that he just rides around in the south part of town. It is a fact that this news disturbs Hodler, but not so much as it excites him. Twister weather. Potential killers. Yet all that Hodler suffers is a pupil dilation, an increase in his pulse. Does he plan to take the twist out of the wind? No, he does not. He plans only to duck it. To use the terms he takes the greatest pains to avoid, it scares the shit out of him, but he likes it. He would gladly take the twist out of that boy who seemed to strike in the same, irresponsible manner, but a twister had obligations that he felt this boy did not. There were these opposing forces, high and low pressures, moist and dry air in unpredictable mixtures, great heat and cold, fantastic combinations that built up like nuclear fission, and most important of all there was the element of chance that dissolved it in vapor, or brought it to perfection, a tube that dipped from the sky and rearranged most of the matter it touched. There were obligations every bit as profound, and more dramatic, than those exercised by Hodler. Each to his own. It was Hodler's obligation to shout and then duck.

Is this why he feels a pleasurable apprehension in the knowledge of this potential killer? Haffner would know that better than Hodler. It is disturbing enough for Hodler to admit it. Destructive elements are not merely on the loose, but some of them are rubbing off on Hodler. It is hardly necessary that he pick up a stranger. They ride with him in the cab. It is still mid-afternoon, but the streets are so dark that lights have come on in many of the houses. They look foolish to Hodler. Do they mean to frighten something off? Hodler lives in the big one with the elm trees at the front, the yellow barn and the sunken creek at the back. In that creek water is running. He hears it at night. The property is Hodler's, but he rents most of it out to a science teacher with a growing family. His wife, a German *hausfrau*, looks after Hodler. Her daughters sprawl on his bed and read his paperback books. They leave the scent of their hairspray on the backs of his chairs, bobby pins in the seat. Hodler can see that the lamps are on in his room, and more than likely his hi-fi tuned to Chicago. The fatter girl is mad for Fritos and salts his pillow as she reads.

The Hodler house features a set of lightning rods ornamented with billiard-size balls of green marble. He has no idea what they do for the lightning but they give character and tone to the house. Several have been chipped by college-boy rifle fire dating before his time. Hodler's property includes a portion of the creek and the strip of lover's lane that runs along beside it, in recent years used only by local dogs and cyclists. If the water is not too high the creek is bridged by a fallen beech tree, belonging to Hodler, or several rotting planks belonging to his neighbor. Children, idlers, and careless or preoc-

123

cupied lovers have fallen off the planks. Hodler's efforts to correct this hazard cost him a lawyer's fee plus the costs for surveying. He was accused of diverting the stream with clear intent to increase his own holdings. The very sight of Hodler so enraged this neighbor she planted a grove of trees to screen off the view of his house, then retired to Florida. The grove has proved a godsend to Hodler, however, since the house is often rented to young people who drink and dance in the patio court. The hi-fi music is supplied by loudspeakers. The house is modern in design, with a flat roof that gleams with water weeks after the rain season, and features walls of tinted glass clear across the back. It is usually leased a year at a time to whomever is new, or transient, at the college, but no matter who it happens to be they forget to drape the glass walls at the back. In the winter they glow like store fronts. Other seasons it is more like a modern stage. The modern stage, in fact, has prepared Hodler for what he often sees through the screen of branches, the public exhibition of relatively private affairs. Hodler has his principles, but he also is human and turns to this prospect as he does to a window. He seldom passes without giving it a glance. The house is currently rented to Alan and Charlotte Hatfield who are fond of cats and music turned up high. They impress Hodler as reasonable people, and the noise is not rudeness, but more that of inexperience. They do not seem to realize how well sound carries in a small, quiet town. Hodler is uncertain whether the husband, the poet, strolls along the creek to get away from the music, or if his wife turns it up so loud to make certain he can hear it where he is walking. In any case Hodler hears it. It is music of the sort that carries, and a little bit of it goes a long way.

From the road Hodler can see the water standing on the roof, and the glow of the lights like a fire at the back. Fortunately Hodler is the nearest neighbor, and what he sometimes witnesses he keeps to himself. Not that it is shocking. But the sort of thing that leads people to talk. Alan will stroll along the creek, where Hodler will see his cigarette glowing, while his very pretty and foreign-looking wife will sometimes dance in the room where the lights are burning and the music throbs. She dances, that is, all by herself. Through the screen of branches Hodler will see her with her arms outspread, her long hair flying, whirling in the manner of a person possessed. This will go on until Alan returns to switch the music off, then jot down the lines he has been brooding. Charlotte will sit by the fire watching him. The music has stopped, but it seems to hover over the scene and be part of its mystery. Strange indeed, Hodler finds it, if not downright peculiar, but also like a scene that a master has painted in a manner long out of fashion. An allegory no less, a tableau with figures both familiar yet mystifying, commonplace yet unreal in the vivid manner of dreams. The poet who walks alone, encased within himself, the dancer who twirls and dances by herself, and the scene that then arranges itself with suggestive but inscrutable commentary. It is this that appeals to Hodler: what escapes. Clowns like Haffner, dreamers like Kashperl, and lovers as strange as the poet Alan and his wife Charlotte. The

125

meaning that escapes exceeds whatever he has grasped. What he seeks lies just beyond the flickering, rain-screened beam of the car lights, the twilight zone that is neither light nor dark. In this light some things are seen at their best. Such light as they have they seem to give out. Road signs, for instance, or the arms of women, or the bobby sox worn by teenagers, or white crash helmets bouncing erratically through a rain-soaked wood. Hodler sees it dimly. He sees it better once the lights are off. It is like many things, but nothing so much as a runaway calf with its head caught in a pail the color of milk. Electrical storms produce puzzling effects, and Hodler can't rule out that this might be one of them. A globe pale but luminous as a street lamp, bouncing through the woods. It comes from the north, where a sparse stand of trees divides the Hodler from the Hatfield property. This creature that is like a calf with a pail on its head stumbles through the brush, then drops from sight. Does a Hodler know a spaceman in orbit when he sees one? It takes him a moment to consider. To see and hear him better he cranks down the window. In the tops of the trees the wind is hollowly moaning. A better word would be coughing, but if Hodler used it he would be considered too literary. The wind is hollowly moaning. The readers of the *Pickett Courier* will agree to that.

Hodler lets the car door hang open while he stoops to grope in the back for his rubbers. The rain has let up, but the grass on the slope will be slick and wet. From the pocket of the door he takes a flashlight with the flickering beam of a candle. He puts it back and takes a handful of matches from the box on the seat. Is it the exercise or the sultry air that films his face? He cranks the window up, closes the vent, backs out, then opens the door to lower both windows an inch or so from the top. One of the problems of the twister is the vacuum at the center causing objects that are sealed up tight to explode. This is twister weather. He has it on good authority. He stands a moment with his eyes on scudding clouds that ill conceal the face of Pauline Bergdahl, or the voice that speaks directly to Hodler. "Who you think gives the twist to the wind, Mr. Hodler, the movie folks?"

A small twist in this wind dips and scoops his hat, then rolls it on its brim, stitched to hold its shape, around the corner of the house and down the slope to where the water runs grass-green around the knees of the man who wades it, slowly, dragging his heavy parcel like a net. The wind scatters a racket that might, or might not, be music, the volume turned up too high. Hodler stands listening, half-dizzy with the noise, his eyes on the slope where the boy stands like a lamp post, the lamp extinguished but aglow with the glare of yellow light from the house. In that glare, if at all, he sees the dancer dimly, and not nearly so well as Hodler, deafened by the music, who takes it all in through his eyes.

Has he known all the time what is happening, who it is that comes riding? The rain in his face is like spray blown from a roaring falls. Light glares on the horizon, but even as he stares it darkens. It has the thick, murky cloudiness of belching smoke. As if Hodler didn't know, he wonders what there is, off there, to burn. Rumbling up behind him there is thunder, but no flash or flicker of lightning. Over across the way the dancer still dances, but the music has stopped. Without waiting for the record on the spindle to drop Hodler is running, or rather he is sliding, filling his lungs with air like water, shouting as he runs, "Run! Run!" then skids and falls.

So far as he knows the boy does nothing. It is Hodler who panics; he sprawls then slides on the oilskin of his slicker, to where he spills, his arms spread wide, into the creek. It is deep enough to float him, his arms thrashing, to where the water flows beneath a culvert, an iron grill beneath it to keep the debris from spilling into the pond. There Hodler is pinned by the force of the water while mountain engines drawing long strings of freight cars cross all the trestles of his life in one deafening roar. Flood, fire and earthquake intermingle, but all of that is hardly new. Even Hodler has suffered it all before, somewhere, with Noah on the ark or with Jonah in the whale's belly, being a man, and subject, like men, to twists in the wind. He will remember the whiteness of the water cupped, like hands, to his ears.

CHAPTER EIGHT

Would you believe that in the beeches near the river he watched this man tie a woman to a tree and take her without taking off his hat? He had a pint bottle of Echo Springs in his pocket and he kept his knees flexed to make sure he wouldn't drop it. When he finished they both went back to picking mushrooms. In the old days, surely, such things were not uncommon, but the times have changed. Nowadays such people would never know toad-stools from mushrooms.

A sleet-like hail pings on his helmet and collects like rice in the seam of his visor. What he needs is a windshield wiper. He laughs. That was also true of the girl he forced. He took her under the bleachers of the Muncie Roller Derby and she bit her own thumb to keep from laughing. In the flesh of her thumb she left her own teeth marks, but she laughed. It hardly matters anymore if you believe it or not: the times have changed.

Is it possible that knavery, thievery, larceny, battery and lechery come naturally to Jubal? How else? It is the only talent he has. It comes to him, more than likely, from his prideful father who wears his red-lined hunting cap at the table, an out-of-date fishing license showing in the vent holes in the crown. His own hand-tied flies are hooked to the brim, and while he eats he rests his chew at the side of his plate, like a gob of grease. His mother's comment has been that if he didn't smell of fish, it might be something worse. One day Jubal will inherit the detachable collars he refuses to wear with the shirts. The stud at the front leaves a green spot on his neck. At Sunday table, in his suit coat, he looks like a cleric. His glasses either reflect the glow of the lamp, or he sits with the light of the sky behind him, a dark figure framed in the open door. Jubal will never know if his eyes are closed while his mother says Grace.

From her he has the black hair, coarse as a mare's tail, the part down the middle like a split in her skull. The bold look she has, the straight look she gives him, may be due to the fact that she has no eyebrows. Never pour kerosene on a bin of smoldering cobs. From that day her skin has been yellow as corn silk, her lips chapped. But she has no fear of fire and will singe a chicken with a flaming newspaper. She likes the burned smell of the hairs on the back of her hand. In the summer she sits and rocks to stir up a draft, using the lap of her apron to fan the air to her face. It is under the square jut of her jaw that she feels the heat. All winter long his mother hooks the afghans that hang on the split-rail fence most of the summer, turned twice a day so they will sun-fade on both sides. People up from Louisville, or down from Muncie, prefer the faded colors because they look old. Other people just stop to take a picture of his mother hand-shelling peas, or popcorn, reclining in the hammock her father made of barrel staves and baling wire. His mother always has to tell them that the peas and the popcorn are not for sale.

Every fall Jubal helps his father pick the pumpkins and pile them in a mound near the road, like wigwams. It is Jubal who sells them. He cleans and carves them with a hunting knife. Waiting for sales he practices chords on his guitar. On Saturday nights he puts the pumpkins around to glow like goblins in the grove of beeches. Those with candles smoke like lanterns, and give off the smell of burned squash. He gets a quarter a piece, along with all the pumpkin pie he can eat.

In the winter the unpainted clapboard house can be seen from the road. It was put up for his mother to be born in, and to serve as a home until they built something better. That was sixty years ago. The trees were cleared to make room for the new foundations, but the stumps are still there. The centers have gone soft, and when Jubal gets warts he dips in his hand to cure them. Barked trees blaze a trail that leads down to the river where the posts of a pier tilt out from the water. Steamers once stopped there. The flap of their paddles churned the water white. Travelers rented horses to ride into Olney where the train made connections to Chicago and Muncie. His mother, Leah Olney, went along just to enjoy the free ride home. That buggy once served Jubal as a playhouse, but now there is nothing left but three wheels. His father used the top to build a lean-to off the house for his bicycle. The house itself is surrounded, like a battlefield, with the wreckage of his father's experiments with farming, a rake and two plows, a corn seeder, the half-moon seat of a weed-buried harrow, the grip on the lever spreading the fingers on a white cotton glove. Wagon wheels without wagons stand in the roofless barn. His father could burn the sideboards, but he could never bring himself to burn the wheels. One of them, with the spokes painted red, is mounted on an axle just off the highway, with the three mailboxes of the Olneys and the Gainers mounted on the rim. Olney County smart alecks pull off the road as they pass just to give it a spin. Whether you believe it or not hardly matters. Even beliefs have changed.

How much does it take to put a boy into orbit who is known to covet another man's wife? Not much. Sometimes no more than the bleat of a horn. The dancer twirls like a swirling scarf: she winds and unwinds like a bolt of cloth. All around them is the sound of a rocket revving up. That seems only fitting, and he is on the pad, his knees flexed, his head dipped low, his lips pursed for the countdown, so the roll of thunder that precedes his blasting off comes as no surprise.

There has been no spring at all, in Charlotte's opinion, and something in the air makes her hair unruly. Alan says it is the storm. He has an explanation for everything. Charlotte would rather that her hair is unruly because it feels that way, as she does. Just before breakfast, when she combed her bangs, the hair rose from her forehead as if drawn by a magnet. She had called to Alan to come and look. Just that walk across the rug gave him such a charge that she got a shock when he touched her.

"Enough in the air to burn the lights," he said.

"Enough what?"

"Electricity. Someday somebody's going to learn how to use it."

"I'm using it now," she said, and held the comb to her bangs.

That was not what Alan meant, of course, and Charlotte's comment did not amuse him. Neither did her call from the pet clinic to come and pick *them* up in Elvira. The weather was foul. It was not uncommon for Charlotte to reflect the moods of the weather, as she did. On a day like this one she would often, as she said herself, cloud up and rain all over him. After the rain, and as suddenly, she would clear up. Charlotte's naïveté is attractive, four out of five times, but the fifth time it is often exasperating. Take her interest in strangers. Her belief that strangers must be interesting. It is idle for Alan to point out that this will disappear the moment she knows them. This interest might flare up, as it usually did, at the most inopportune moment. It is hardly Charlotte's fault, of course, if Alan chooses to park at a very peculiar parking meter: one that is already occupied by an army duffle and a guitar.

Whose were they? She simply had to know. It was just the sort of thing that fascinated Charlotte, and naturally that is just what happened. Fascination. Nothing else on

133

her mind. Alan had made the stop to pick up some groceries, and on their way home they passed this boy on the highway, soaked with the rain. *That* was him. She was absolutely certain. How did she know? She *knew*. This kid would be with them now, drying off by the fire, giving off the strong smell of boots and wet leather, sipping some of Alan's Duff Gordon sherry, if the boy hadn't proved to be as sensible and suspicious as Alan. "No thanks," he said, when offered the lift, much to Alan's relief. On the very day some rapist or delinquent was known to be loose on the streets of Pickett, Charlotte *would* be determined to give him a lift.

Alan has a reflective turn of mind that helps him live in Pickett, but is no help with Charlotte. Anything at all might interest Alan. It has to be *alive* to interest Charlotte. In her opinion, not many of the people in Pickett are. If people asked her why she likes cats Charlotte will say that she likes something alive around her. She doesn't mean Alan isn't alive. But cats don't think. After one year in Pickett she prefers creatures who don't think.

Charlotte herself is alive in a way electricity is, and it makes her unruly. On certain days, like this one, she seems charged with it. Alan is both pleased and disturbed by the sight of it. After all, it is why he loves her, and he would rather live with it than do without it. But it is not easy. She is alive in a way that most people are not. In his career, for instance, it has led to friction, and delayed his promotion in the English department. They both admit that's a small point, but there it is. Charlotte would like to spend another year or two in Perugia where they lived on

Italian brandy and pizza, but without a promotion it is hard to arrange. The Italians suit Charlotte. Without one word of the language she gets along fine.

In Pickett, Alan is either too hot or too cold, and sits around the house with his hands in his pockets. He has found he likes the smell of leaves burning, but the taste of fresh snow bitter. His mother writes from Florida that the taste of old-time snow was sweet. Alan lets his hair grow longer than he should because the barbers in Pickett always cut it too short. They cannot seem to grasp what Alan seems to mean by full around the ears. Something in the air, or something not in it, makes Charlotte's hair hard to manage, and Alan uses a menthol-flavored chapstick on his lips. Charlotte doesn't like anything medicated, and always wipes Alan's lips off before she will kiss him. Charlotte doesn't actually dislike Pickett, but she would rather live where she can get groceries delivered. Not that she minds shopping. She simply can't stand fat-assed women in shorts with shopping carts. Alan is accustomed to help with the shopping but he can't be trusted with the cat food. He buys mackerel, and the cats won't eat it. On rainy days they usually grill steaks in the fireplace, but today it is too windy, and Charlotte has read that charcoal smoke is poisonous. Alan has tried to explain that if the draft is open most of this gas will go up the chimney. His mistake was using the word gas. That is why the patio door stands open and Kid Ory's horn, if not the "Mecca Flat Blues," can be heard by their neighbors. If the hour is late Alan will ask Charlotte to please be reasonable—but the hour is not late. Dark as it is, it is just past five. Alan knows that Dr. Bohlen, a professor of history, now sits at the dark window of his study, a glass of sherry in his hand, watching Charlotte dance. A bird fancier, he uses high-powered German bird glasses. Alan has often seen him, owl-eyed, at the window he lowers from the top. He gives Alan furtive glances of envy and distaste when they pass in the hall. Dr. Bohlen is no more nor less a lecher than most men, but he has no way of judging a woman like Charlotte. Who has? Alan has been working at it for years. One of the fancies he often has, while listening, deafened, to the music, is that he sees the phantom dancer who comes out of the horn to dance with Charlotte. Yet it is no lover. It is nothing but the dance itself. When Charlotte cries, "You hear that horn?" Alan seldom hears it, but he often sees it, a force that vibrates the bell of the horn and takes possession of his wife. It is not pretty. It is seldom happy. Neither does it burn with a gem-like flame, but whatever it is that burns loves the fire. Alan is merely a poet. How does he know if it is the dinner he smells burning, or his wife?

The room is dark. Water drips on the logs in the fireplace. It both pleases and disturbs Alan to see her pawing through the phonograph records. They are old ones, they belong to Charlotte, and some of them were pretty worn back when they were married. The music is not exactly to Alan's taste, but the bands are good. For reasons Alan has never quite fathomed Charlotte's idea of jazz is the old-time jazz. Bob Scobey's Frisco band is as modern as she cares to get. Kid Ory is Charlotte's idea of a really great horn man, and "Mecca Flat Blues" is her idea of a really great tune. Not that Alan disagrees. But a little of the old stuff goes a long way. Alan prefers the cool side of jazz if the evening is going to be a long one. All he asks is that Charlotte be reasonable. But once Charlotte gets a load of Kid Ory's horn she is not a reasonable Charlotte. She will jump up and cry, "Man, dig that horn!" Once she is up, it is hard to get her down. She likes to dance with Alan, but even better she likes to dance by herself. Either way she is good. Alan prefers to sit with a book, or the whiskey carton containing the first draft of his thesis, working on the index while Kid Ory blows and Charlotte dances. Sometimes she doesn't seem to mind. Sometimes she does. The old-time jazz is not background music: Kid Ory blows his horn to make a good time. If Alan just sits there, preoccupied, Charlotte might turn up the volume until the windows rattle. If he glances up at her she will say, "He's the greatest! Can't you hear that horn?"

Alan's usual reply is that he couldn't: no, he couldn't, since the racket actually deafened him. There was truth in that. The speakers in the system have more than forty watts of power. Alan can see the music better than he can hear it through the fabric that covers the front of the speakers: the coil of the speaker is like the vibrating bell of Kid Ory's horn. Alan is not blind to Kid Ory's talent, but he does find the volume disturbing. Charlotte, of course, has turned up the volume to make sure he can hear. If he *really* can hear, he will get up and dance. It's not a point that discussion clears up, and with the volume up there is no discussion. Charlotte dances. Alan sits with his book. Is it possible to say he no longer sees the dancer, only the dance?

He gets up, taking his empty glass with him as he walks

into the kitchen. A leg of lamb is roasting. An alarm on the stove will buzz when it is done. Alan fishes several ice cubes from the tray in the sink, pours over them two fingers of rye whiskey. He stands dunking the cubes with one finger as he watches the storm. A sleeting hail pings on the window like a handful of rice, as it was also pinging on a white crash helmet. For how many thousands of years had squares like Alan wondered about non-squares seen along the highway? And for how many thousand years had squares like Alan said sobering things to girls like Charlotte? For less than fifty they could turn and put a record on the Gramophone.

A sudden draft reminds Alan that a door must be open and he walks down the hall to their bedroom. The patio door stands open. The half-drawn drapes are wet. Water glistens like oil on the floor near the bed. Through the splattered window Alan sees the plants shining like tin, the leaves grease-spotted. He no longer believes most plants are real. The window frames a dark scene that is elegantly balanced by the lights at the Bohlens', and a slicker that seems to hang from a branch near the creek. After a moment Alan sees that a man stands within it. A cap shields his face. He has stopped along the path to fill his eyes with Charlotte. Alan could put a stop to this by pulling the drapes but that is precisely what he'd rather not do. It would imply that *they* were right in their thinking, and *they* were wrong. And it would be what they couldn't see that would lead them to talk. The upstairs windows of the Bohlen house are dark, but lights burn on the glassed-in porch. Mrs. Bohlen has her hands full of the grandchildren she baby-sits for her two married daughters. Alan often hears them squalling. The oldest daughter, a tall, straight-limbed girl who looked very good at a distance, was the mother of the twins in the pram. In the window corner, under one of the bridge lamps, another child lies on its back, waving its arms and legs. It is strapped to a pallet shaped like a flour scoop, a device made to order for the suburban papoose. Alan had seen them in the seats of cars, or in the carts and baskets at supermarkets. He is amused by the frog-like kick of the tiny bowed legs. Where did it think it was? Or better yet, what? Fish or frog below the hips, what was it above? The stubby arms jerked spasmodically, the head rocked from side to side. No rhythm to it, no meaning to it, just a pointless, mindless movement: Alan thinks of weeds caught in the windslip of a car. From wherever these limbs took their orders, what did they think they were doing? It amused Alan to note that the kick of the legs seemed in time to Charlotte's dance music. The child did not hear it, loud as it was, but in its nerves a similar pulse was beating. The dance that preceded the music. The beat preceding the dance.

In a dentist's chair, the apparatus at rest while the novocain worked its spell on him, Alan had been given a copy of *Life* featuring X-ray photographs of unborn babies. He saw only one. The unborn child, months away from birth, away from the passions and corruptions of this world, blindly sucked its thumb. Before it knew the pleasures and purposes of sucking this womb-trapped infant suckled. Before it heard music, there was a tingling

139

dance along the nerves. In the blood that coursed the veins, tracing a leaf-like pattern, a blueprint for the wondrous work of man, music coursed before the ear had been shaped to hear. What had not been *given?* What could not be described as an inheritance? *The keys to. Given! A way a lone a last a loved a long the riverrun, past Eve and Adam's, from swerve of shore to bend of bay, brings us by a commodius vicus of recirculation back to Howth Castle and* the room where Charlotte dances. Between Alan and this room there is an outdoor patio and several redwood benches. The rain has brought out the color in the patio tiles, but with a shift in the wind the rain has stopped. A squall-like breeze blows in Alan's face. The figure standing to the left of the outdoor grill is so much like an object Alan is not startled. The helmet gleams like a bucket left to drain on a post, or crown a piece of garden statuary. How long has *it* been there? The narrow shoulders are darkly wet. One arm dangles an object that seems to anchor the figure in place. It stands with its back to Alan, facing the room where Charlotte is dancing, twirling slowly now, like a dying top. In a moment she will fall, or thump into something, but it is strange how fatigue makes her buoyant, as if an invisible arm supports her at the waist. Her head lolls. Her hands droop as if her wrists were clamped in stocks. In a moment she will fall, but he stands watching this mute figure watch the dance. He wonders how it must look through the stranger's eyes. It seems to Alan, sheltered in the doorway, that the figure and the dancer symbolize something, an allegory in the manner of the Old Masters, actors caught at that precise moment the play or the parable reveals its meaning. Does it charm him to the extent that it escapes him? The dying dance, the fading horn, the froglike kicking of the child's legs, and the figure that broods in the wings of the scene, like Alan himself.

A suck of wind, cool on Alan's damp back, puffs the curtains of his study and they flap in the doorway. One fills like a sail, then blows loose like the cloak of someone fleeing. That might be Alan, but it is more in the likeness of Charlotte. A winged spirit leaving a troubled house. Papers lift from his desk and strew the floor in the manner that she prefers to strew them. She does not like papers. She does not like the thought, or the poem, that submits to typing. She does not like the music until it becomes the dance.

Papers blow into the court like uncaged birds, several lift and flap like headless chickens. It is not like Alan to stand like a dreamer, but he feels it is part of the scene he is recording. Wind, rain and the fitful movement of things that blow. Trees sweep the clouds with the sound of egg beaters, but it does not occur to Alan to question what he hears. Lights blink on and off. He hears glass shatter and the slam of doors. He hardly knows, or cares, if the flash he sees is in the air or in his head. Whether he falls or is blown into the closet, where he drags clothes from the hooks and hangers, it is there, in the muffled silence, he finds himself. The roof has been peeled from his study and the bed is stripped to the mattress. The door is gone from the hall, and he goes down it to find Charlotte wrapped in drapes that have been torn from the windows,

141

her cheeks rain-splattered. Calling her name does nothing. He has to shake her awake.

"Where is he?" she cries.

Of course he says, "He who?"

"He was here. Right there——!" but nobody is there where she wags her finger, or much of anything else. The redwood benches and tables, the striped umbrella, the hood to the outdoor grill, the mattress for sunbathing: gone. Nor hide nor hair of *him*—whoever he was. "He was there. Right there. I saw him!"

"Sure, sure," says Alan, and kneels stroking her forehead. When the wind is on the loose, as he can testify, people are subject to seeing strange things. The roof is torn, but the windows are intact through which he sees the approaching car lights, the revolving beacon, and the spotlight that sweeps the scene. By some caprice of nature —as he will later describe it—the twister lifted the roof, as from a doll's house, leaving the room relatively undisturbed, the updraft of wind blowing alive the coals in the fireplace. It was like they were under the open sky, camping out on the beach. That's what it was like if you were like Alan, with a poet's turn of speech.

Mrs. Bohlen will describe it, understandably, as less a caprice of nature than an act of God. The twister veered around the Bohlen house, giving it a wrenching twist on the cinder-block foundation, but hardly disturbing the children in the basement or the child who thrashed its legs on the pallet. Still acting for God it then hopped the Library, flattened the jerry-built structure just behind it, then left untouched the dormitory where sixty-five sophomore girls were taking showers, cramming for exams, or just waiting for boys. The building suffered no more than the loss of several awnings, put up in anticipation of the summer weather, and a metal rack occupied by several scooters and something more than forty-five bicycles. Most of the girls went to dinner not knowing that a twister had struck next door.

That is not true of Hodler, who will make, in time, his own eye-witness report. He will owe to Avery such details that his life was saved by his yellow slicker. Air trapped in its sleeves, transforming them to water wings, and the bubble of air ballooning at the back, supported Hodler in the culvert until he was spotted by eagle-eyed Avery, one of Fire Chief Maynard's experienced assistants in rescue work. The spotlight panning this scene, the trees debarked or uprooted, the trunks that held on but had lost their upper branches, like roots clutching at the air or hands with broken, gnarled fingers—this light picked up the glint of Hodler's yellow slicker where he was piled with the debris beneath the culvert, almost as bright as a stop sign, as Avery put it himself. Avery was especially pleased to be the one to find Hodler, since he had a news tip that wouldn't wait. Miss Holly had been assaulted, but not too well raped, since there wasn't much sign of penetration. The criminal had to settle for a good-sized bite of you-know-what. That news did more for Avery, who panted hoarsely as he told it, than it seemed to do for

143

Hodler, who heard it with his slicker pockets weighted with water and his corduroy cap shrinking on his wet head. Perhaps it restored, for Avery, something of Miss Holly's market value as an item somewhat shopworn, but still unused.

Although the poet's house still stands, with a bed dry enough to sleep in, a fire in the grate, and food in the icebox, Alan thought it might be better to stay in a motel and check Charlotte in at the clinic. There was a chance of shock. She was still in a somewhat confused state of mind. Alan himself would also like to help those who had not come out of it as luckily as they had.

The bad spots were Scampi's Bar, on Route 7, and Mrs. Bergdahl's diner. A dozen people or more had been seated at the counter when some fool ran in and shouted, "A twister! A twister!" All but two of them had run outside and been blown away, or struck by something. Pauline Bergdahl had had the presence of mind to break half the windows by throwing plates at them. A tree had fallen on the diner, but nobody inside had been hurt. At Scampi's Bar and Cafe the men seated at the bar had gone through the trapdoor in the floor behind it. Otherwise nothing remained but the gas pumps at the front. Five cars had been parked there: none had been found. Choice bottles of whiskey and brandy were strewn in adjoining fields of soybeans and alfalfa. Two women dead. Both had been in the ladies' room at the back.

It is Alan who comments that the scene itself is too familiar a spectacle to be tragic. Debarked trees, fragments of buildings, chimneys that stand like grave markers, have been seen by everybody in actual war, or in peace at the movies. One's first thought is "What is it like? What does it remind me of?"

"I'm not reminded of *anything*," Charlotte says. Looking at her—she is draped in a blanket courtesy of Kashperl's Army & Navy Surplus—Hodler is reminded that women *are* different from men. Her bare flat feet look blue. Her hair hangs like a rain-drenched squaw. Could he with assurance say that this woman, just twenty minutes past, danced as if possessed? It seemed unlikely. Most people would say that he was seeing things. Hodler too, the yellow slicker removed, is given a blanket to wrap around his shoulders, the smell of the mothballs having a slightly tonic effect. He has lost one shoe. Only now does he notice that fact. With Charlotte and Alan—Charlotte folded between them—he is put into the back seat of Maynard's car, a souped-up Chevy painted the color of luminous bobby sox. The emblem of the Fire Chief is painted on the door. Avery and Maynard take seats in front, where the radio squawks news of the disaster. A dozen or more people are known to be missing. Are Hodler, Charlotte, and Alan three of them? Maynard comments that some of the kids in Pickett had more up-to-date equipment to play with than he had: with a walkie-talkie he could make his report and help clear matters up.

Fallen trees have blocked the road back to the square, so they go along the creek drive toward the highway. High on one of the trees, like a Christmas ornament, hangs a bicycle. Hodler thinks that is new, *that* belongs to this scene and not something he has seen in the movies. Sanford Avery, however, begs to take exception. He has seen it before. Not a bicycle but a tassel-fringed buggy as if the people had gone for a sky ride. Up there for weeks, since they had no hook and ladders to get it down. Avery speaks eagerly but a little hoarsely: the disaster has aroused his nostalgia. The twisters of today are not to be compared with the twisters of the past. Just as an example —had Hodler ever seen fireballs rolling down the street like cartwheels? No, he hadn't. Well, that was what Avery meant. Fireballs in his youth were commonplace. They would roll along the road until they hit a tree or something, then they would explode. Something to do with electricity, more than likely, which also might explain things no longer heard of. Plain straw, chaff from the barn floor, driven through planks like so many nails. Avery had seen it. One of the commonplace wonders of the past. With his own eyes from where he lay in a storm cave—did Charlotte know what a storm cave was, no, she didn't—but Avery crouched in one, the door torn off so he could see a chunk of the sky, and up there he saw a horse go swimming by with the harness trailing. It might have been, but wasn't, the horse previously hitched to that buggy left in the tree. This horse swam by like the air was water using something like a side-kick, his mane flying, his eyes bulging, and still wearing part of his harness. That same storm blew a silo across the river and rolled it down the field like a barrel. He, Avery, was grateful for having lived at a time when the storms were still great, like this one. They would break up a man like ice in a sack and at the same time leave his watch still ticking. The power in such a twister was peculiarly awesome because you couldn't tell where it might strike next. Only God knew that.

"You can say that again," says Maynard.

Alan says, "If we could harness all that power——" but he stops there to put his arm around Charlotte. Her head is wagging, strands of her wet hair whip Hodler's face.

"Harness! Harness!" she cries. "You and your harness-ing!"

Hodler is grateful the cab is dark. He feels the body of Charlotte stiffen, then relax. Alan holds a piece of tissue to her nose, says, "Blow."

Maynard says, "Now where the hell we at?" and flicks on his brighter lights. They are just east of Scampi's corner, but Scampi's is gone. The gas pumps—it seems to Hodler—stand like symbolic figures of mourning, some-thing new in Pop art.

"Gone with the wind!" barks Avery. "Now how about that?"

There is no comment. Maynard spins the wheel and they follow Route 7 back into town. They listen to the news on the hour, the volume turned up. Five are now known to be dead, eleven missing, but the worst seems to be over. Between Pickett and Libby the twister dissolved into thin air.

Hodler is thinking of that boy with his arms spread wide who came riding as if about to be shot into orbit. What did he make of events that made so much, or so little, of him? In describing him as a spaceman, perhaps

Miss Holly had him accurately spotted. On the radar screen a spaceman and a twister left the same track. Both were in orbit, or out of it, according to Kashperl's Law. It occurs to Hodler that the events of this day, like the wreckage strewn by the twister, were already being assembled according to the needs of the survivors. Sense for Hodler, nonsense for Haffner, for Pauline the way God's cookie crumbles, for the man on the loose one more twist in the tail of the wind.

"Who's that?" says Avery.

In the beam of the lights a figure stands with one foot in the road. His head and feet are bare. The portrait on his chest is like a color-running tattoo. The car's revolving beacon makes a blob of his face, the eyes gleaming like the gems in road signs. Hodler has seen such faces before, crawling from the sea at Anzio, the obligations stripped away, the choice residing in a twist of the wind. Does he mean to hitch a ride? As if awakened from sleep Charlotte's body stiffens, the hand lifts from her lap and frantically waves. Then she leans forward to give a long toot on Maynard's horn. Not unlike Charlotte, it seems to Hodler, one of the boy's long arms flings into the air, spilling water from the helmet he loops like a bucket to splatter the hood of the car and the windshield, then drops to slap at his side.

"Who the hell——" says Maynard. They are startled by Charlotte's shrill laughter. She leans over the seat toward the rearview mirror, which she tips to see the road behind her. Hodler, too, sees the white helmet, tinted by the glow from the rear lights, loop in the air like a warning signal without its clanging bell. The arm of Charlotte thumps Hodler's cap as she waves.

"Could we drop by the clinic, Mr. Maynard?" asks Alan.

"Can if it's still there," Maynard replies.

The traffic lights are still out at the intersection where smoking red flares are hissing, and Alan slips his arm around the shoulders of his laughing wife.

CHAPTER NINE

Hodler sleeps. He is hardly a man of pent-up emotions, but after any bad storm he sleeps like a baby. The worse the storm, the better he sleeps. Somthing in his nature, as well as in nature, seems to find release. His landlady is under orders to wake him at seven, but this clear, cool morning she lets him sleep. One shoe dries in the kitchen. His wet clothes hang where they can drip in the tub.

It is always Haffner's luck to sleep through the twisters, then wake up safe and sound and read about it in the papers. This morning there are no pictures in the *Pickett Courier*, but a note to the effect that the prediction proved accurate. *Twister weather, chances for rain 80%*. One of Hodler's checks will go off to Pauline Bergdahl in the early mail.

Kashperl daydreams. His nurse, Miss Boyle, has opened the blinds so he can see for himself that the town is still there. Not all of it, however. The historic elm is gone, but a wedge is on display in the Pickett Inn. Personalized wedges, bearing the college seal, are available on order from the alumnae secretary. In Miss Boyle's frank opinion many people will buy one to remember the twister, rather than the college, or the day the juvenile delinquent was on the loose. Little is known about him beyond the fact that he is juvenile.

While Miss Boyle chatters Kashperl daydreams of unrelated matters. How once he crouched, like an egg in its cup, to scan the volumes in a basket priced at 10¢. As he browsed another man's feet appeared at his side. They were large, pavement-flattened city feet in a pair of battered, world-weary shoes. Ashes from a cigar occasionally dropped to the brim of Kashperl's hat. The floorboards creaked as the man shifted his weight. Kashperl remained crouched, like a thief in a cornfield, while this reader sampled volumes from the upper shelves. Like Kashperl he dipped into them at random. From one, without warning, he intoned—

Ah, what a dusty answer gets the soul
When hot for certainty in this our life.

Kashperl made no sign. The finger of God might have written this message on the wall of his mind. A dusty answer. Vintage pathos for Kashperl's soul. The man who spoke these words then creaked off ignorant of what he had done to Kashperl. Hot for certainties in this our life, Kashperl a collector of dusty answers. It was no accident the author remained anonymous.

The big wind has not disturbed the Stohrmeyer house but it departed with most of the leghorn chickens, not one of the sickly Plymouth Rocks. How explain it? Avery can hardly wait for Hodler to get to his office. TWISTER

151

PICKS GOOD HENS FROM BAD ON STOHRMEYER FARM. Looking for the eggs, Avery has found an old hen with a brood of chicks. She follows him, the chirping brood trailing, across the pitted yard to where Miss Holly sits in her rocker coring apples. Not an apple was touched. Already bees hover over the peelings in her lap, and swarm in a cloud above the roofless porch.

Early this morning Emil Bergdahl, his nightshirt tucked into his pants, served coffee to a kid who had run out of gas. In Bergdahl's opinion his wife had done more damage than the wind. Through the windows she had smashed he could see the banners still waving between the gas pumps, and the coon tail dangling from the handlebars of one motorbike. Two others were gone. There's no accounting for a twist in the wind. The kid with the dented helmet paid for his coffee and two packets of chocolate cupcakes, but he left his guitar as deposit on four gallons of gas. He gets eighty to the gallon, if he first gets the gallon into the tank.

████

That's the picture: there are those who can take it in at a glance. This boy now goes riding with his arms sucked in, his tight-assed pants glued to the saddle. There is no longer much flex in his knees, much spring in his legs. The words of a song do not trail out behind him like the tail of a kite. The levis stretch and fade on the rack of his thighs and his flesh is the color of sun-dried laundry. If travel broadens, why is it everything else shrinks? The shark-toothed jaws of the zipper gleam at his open fly. On his chest J. S. Bach dries in a manner that enlarges his forehead, curves his lips in a smile. Is that for what looms up ahead, or lies behind? This boy is like a diver who has gone too deep and too long without air. If the army is no place for a growing boy, neither is the world. Bombed out are all of the bridges behind him, up ahead of him, treeless, loom the plains of China, the cops, LeRoy Cluett, and the sunrise on the windows of the Muncie Draft Board. There is no place to hide. But perhaps the important detail escapes you. He is in motion. Now you see him, now you don't. If you pin him down in time he is lost in space. Somewhere between where he is from and where he is going he wheels in an unpredictable orbit. He is as free, and as captive, as the wind in his face. In the crown of his helmet are the shoes of a dancer with one heel missing, one strap broken. Such things come naturally to knaves, dancers, lovers and twists of the wind. This cool spring morning the rain-scoured light gleams on his helmet, like a saucer in orbit, where the supernatural is just naturally a part of his life.